DRIVING IN CARS
WITH HOMELESS MEN

DRUE HEINZ LITERATURE PRIZE

# DRIVING
## IN CARS WITH
# HOMELESS
# MEN

## KATE WISEL

University of Pittsburgh Press

Published by the University of Pittsburgh Press, Pittsburgh, Pa., 15260
Copyright © 2019, Kate Wisel

Manufactured in the United States of America
Printed on acid-free paper
10 9 8 7 6 5 4 3 2 1

ISBN 13: 978-0-8229-4568-0
ISBN 10: 0-8229-4568-1

Cataloging-in-Publication data is available from the Library of Congress

Cover photo: Stephen Gill/Gallery Stock
Cover design: Catherine Casalino

But the way it happens sometimes
is that pain becomes a feed for courage,
a nutrient for it: when pain drips
steadily, it can embolden.

KEVIN BARRY, "LAST DAYS OF THE BUFFALO"
*THERE ARE LITTLE KINGDOMS*

# CONTENTS

# DRIVING IN CARS
# WITH HOMELESS MEN

# US

# HOOPS

**WHEN THE COPS CAME,** they came to find us. We huddled by the glittering green sign that said No Loitering. Mozart Park after midnight, on the sidelines in our long-ass sleep tees, watching the boys make free throws in the dark. We were fourteen. We had stubbed butts in our pockets and no curfews.

They'd find us at the packie because we sat with our arms linked on the semi-circle stoop. The alkies strutted past, their beards streaks of dirt. We snickered as we rolled crushed Altoids into computer paper. The taste, burnt and crispy, flying up between our lips. Or in the Best Buy parking lot, where we kicked up cartwheels into parked cars. Screamed "O-B-G-Y-N!" to the ladies making their way through the automatic doors, their purses clutched to their sides. On the rocks, we licked the chocolate crusts of Reese's. Shards of glass in our foam sandals. The clouds sat close. We were roofless. We got bored with the sky and collected trash like criminals. A collage of wet Colt 45 wrappers, warped pages from nudies. Blond girls with their eyes scratched off, their mouths dropped above tits that suffocated their necks.

October we were older. We knew Fetus from the park, where he practiced his amateur boxing. He took us to his garage, where there was a white fridge and a pool table and a concrete floor that smelled like sharp tools. We poured liters of

Smirnoff into a watermelon, then shook the chunky liquor in cans of orange soda from Nemo's. Fetus had sticky, thin lips like the gleam of Smirnoff on the rinds. He'd crouch crow-like on the stool, chalking his cue. He shelled out Oxys like they were mints. The faded shamrock on his neck was a voyeur, a pale green cloud.

One night his mother shuffled in with a greasy ponytail and rhinestone jeans loose like on the rack. She asked us for a lip gloss. In a blurry picture from a disposable camera, she tried to pose with us. Stretched across the green felt, she looked at home among us. We wore hoodies and lip rings, gold hoops that turned our earlobes green. Neon safety vests with no bras. Our pupils pinpointed and bloodshot but shining with purple shadow when the flash caught our blink.

The cops drove slowly down Fetus's snowy side street. They waited for the snap of a match in the front yard. For a cackle to crack out of the dark. They stood sideways with their shoulders against the garage door, shining flashlights, rapping their knuckles with muscle. They had a sweet tooth for knocking. We squatted behind the torn floral couch as they swarmed, our feet ready as springs. We darted, deft as light. We climbed Fetus's stairs to tear open the attic window. We pulled each other out like baby teeth, then skidded our butts down the icy roof. We jumped, all four at once. In the patch of snow, an emergency of laughter, one hairline fracture. We were already gone when the track switched and Biggie chuckled: "Fuck all you hos! Get a grip!"

We waited for one another. In the Intrepid outside English High, at the 7-Eleven, outside stalls, the faucet dripping away seconds. We took just as much, ran just as fast, just as far. There were no gardens to trample, planted pathways of blue and purple. Just the rattle of the chain-link after we jumped it.

Winter was a wall we couldn't see beyond till the garage door moaned when Fetus pulled it, the sky above the triple-deckers dripping colors like splat fruit. If you touched us, we shivered. Our skin like tangerines, on the cusp of bursting.

By spring, the sun vicious on the seats, we were sitting sweaty in the Impala, its rust spots like psoriasis. We circled the Burger King lot, waiting for Fetus. We'd skipped tests, joined zero teams. We didn't fling ourselves around a track field after the crack of a gunshot. Next spring, in the same BK lot, we heard a cop found some girl in the back seat of a hoopty. He shook her shoulders, shot a vial of Narcan up her nose. She was blacked out, the tips of her fingers ice, so blue they were white.

The dark came every night. Summer came without asking. We were back on the rocks, stumbling, pocketing curled-up candy wrappers fallen from our fingers one whole summer back. Poised to plummet into the woods' dark center. And beyond the tips of trees, the Boston skyline looked tiny as a postcard in the window of a gift shop we were once kicked out of. The cops never caught us, held our wrists, kept us in their firm, disingenuous, fatherly grips. There was nowhere to sit, so we sat on the rocks, the bright blue thirties, each other. We were skin-close to the sky. Our cheeks against that torn black sheet.

# SERENA

# FRANKIE

**"YOU LIKE BAD BOYS."** That's what Frankie says.

I used to date a guy with stab wounds on his shoulder I traced in bed while he slept, raised white dashes like the tick of highway lanes. Bad like with toothpicks between their teeth. Idiots really, the kind who wore black hats backward with no logo, walked with a limp, fucked with their tongue out, dropped out of high school, worked at the Sunoco, or security, and got me in for free.

Guys who would text me *what up* and when I said *nothing, you?* I never heard back. I liked it when they disrespected their mothers. Or picked me up after school, then dropped me off somewhere discreet, like the back parking lot of a movie theater. I liked them for short, ballistic bursts, so much that if I crossed the street I'd get hit.

I got over boys and went for older guys instead: an investment banker, lawyers, one with three kids and one who kept blueberries in the console of his BMW, a fad diet. In the sunlight, I could see his every pore. He was late for a meeting, so everything was quick. He told me my hips looked like a Coke bottle, and my ass, bent over, a heart. Once he grabbed my cheeks and knocked my head back onto the metal pole in his condo. I liked to press that soft spot behind my ponytail, the dull ache, days later when I was spaced out at the register.

These were the kinds of men with magazine subscriptions that I flipped through on the train home, licking my finger to flip the thin pages that smelled like the inside of a wooden treasure chest. The last one bought me Summer Jam tickets, one for me and one for Frankie. Frankie went anyway, even though she said, "No clue he was married? Let's think of a more original lie."

Frankie could pick a guy out of a lineup even if she wasn't the witness. That's what she does: picks. We live together in a two-bedroom split above Sal's Pizza, where the dopeheads blabber beneath our open windows at night. Sometimes, when I can't sleep, I crawl into her bed. She lies on her side with her head propped in her palm, her sheets smelling like a department store with the sweet soak of her Guess perfume.

It's confession, lying there in the dark while Frankie listens. Wrought iron shadows from branches partition the sheet as she points sturdy words like vectors toward my heart. She knows things. She majors in Human Development. That means something to her since we both dropped out of school our first semester, failing being my specialty, then reenrolled the next fall. I don't really care about school, specifically the part when men walk in and try to educate me.

Sunday and we're curled into the velvet couch we carried all the way from Goodwill ourselves, then pushed into the corner of our old, enormous kitchen. When I brought this guy Andrew home the first time, I dragged him to my bedroom as Frankie flashed a thumbs-up from the couch. She tells me she likes him because he has natural blond hair and an office job downtown, and takes me to dinner like a real guy. We met in what Frankie calls "a picturesque way." This is the thing: ever since Frankie's mom died, she wants everything to go right.

"How did it go?" Frankie says. I'm wearing a softball tee that got mixed up in the laundry and belongs to Frankie. Frankie's wearing a button-up sweater and a smile that belongs in toothpaste commercials.

"He took me out for Chinese," I start. I pass back the gravity bong we fashioned from a Pepsi bottle. Her cheekbones flush with rosacea, which makes her look possessed by insider information, like someone's got their mouth to her ear.

"Details," she says.

It goes more or less like this: Andrew reached his hands across the booth just as I was about to say, "I have an early dentist appointment in the morning." The waiter moved to our table with the purposefulness of a surgeon and filled our water, shard-like ice cubes cracking in the silence. Then the food came, platter by platter, clouds of steam swooshing into our faces. I filled my plate and drowned my rice in duck sauce.

"You must have been hungry," he said as I scraped the last grains with my fork. "Do you want to order dessert?" He leaned forward with the enthusiasm of a talk show host. I ordered another Blue Moon. By the time he got the check I was almost lying down corpse-like in the booth. I stared at him sleepily, exaggerating my blink like a housecat. I contemplated burping but foresaw him refusing the check and thought better of it. Instead, I reached across the table and crushed a fortune cookie in my fist. I straightened up to pick the fortune from the remains, which read: *You need only to understand that it is not necessary it understand but only enjoy.*

He insisted on walking me home. He tried again to hold my hand as we moved under streetlights that lit up our faces like morons at a spelling bee in which we knew none of the words. I let him grasp my forefinger, which only made me blush.

"Careful," he said as I kicked my way through the broken glass of me and Frankie's block, jellied condoms lying shriveled in the cracks. We passed the methadone clinic by Packard's Corner, where beyond the parking lot the registered sex offenders live in tighter and tighter clusters of red dots like the clap. I was stumbling drunk, and hoped he would leave me at my front door without asking to come inside.

When he did, I said, in my best robot, "I do not have air conditioning."

We stood in the envelope-littered foyer as he watched me stab keys into my lock. When the door swung open I held my hand on the knob while he waved, tripping down a step as he reversed his way out of my sight.

But I don't tell Frankie this. I just say, "It's not going to work out."

She makes a face, taking the bong between her knees. "This is my last one," she says. Later on, she wants to study for the first test of senior year. She's been spending more time in her room, taking notes from textbooks under the clicky green lamp we took from our neighbor's moving van. Last week, when we were in line at Shaw's, I was flipping through an *Us Weekly*, and she said, "You know what's weird? I think I could actually be a psychologist."

"Okay," I said, my nail hooked to my tooth. "Calm down, though."

She pulls a small hit, the lit aluminum speckled with holes from a safety clip. She watches me as I watch her suck the smoke between her teeth. When she exhales, it vanishes up her nostrils as she bends to put the bong back on the windowsill.

"I thought he liked you," she says in a strained voice, coughing emphatically with my bad-luck white lighter clenched in her fist. "I thought things were good," she says again after a long pause.

I dig for explanations: I need space. He's not my type. He calls me "Miss Serena." I don't like his name. *Andrew.* So kindergarten name tag. Like his parents are still together, paid for his college, take a knee in Christmas cards. Go through his iPod and tell me there's not a Blues Traveler playlist. He probably strolls into work in some you're-gonna-love-the-way-you-look-I-guarantee-it fuckin' suit."

I catch Frankie looking at me like I've turned down the wrong road in my mind only to find her standing there on the other side, tapping her foot.

When Frankie and I first met freshman year of high school, we were both locked out of the basement storm doors of a frat party on purpose. Frankie had a gleaming lip ring that gave her wide eyes a lost but poised look. She was drenched from a forty that got poured over her head, I assumed, for being beautiful.

"Do you smoke?" she asked. Her voice had the sageness of a runaway. I had never had a friend who was a girl. She touched my hand.

"Watch," she said as she pulled a cigar from her pocket.

Some people remember things like their first kiss. I remember this: us sitting against the shingles of the frat house, our knees up against our chests. *Haa-haa*, she went, fogging the emptied paper up with her breath like she was trying to keep warm. Then she licked around the tatty edges and sealed the blunt with her lighter, sticking it carefully between my lips. Like that, a candle between us when Frankie clicked. The flame lit her face, a ghost story, her eyebrows darkly arched and expectant.

She said, "Real light, just a little bit."

I look past her head at the ripped-up billboard that levels with our window. Sometimes it feels like we're waking up to the same morning, weekend after weekend, the billboard the only thing that changes. Frankie asking me how things went, her red-brown hair wet like leaves down her shoulders.

Frankie, despiser of ambivalence, saying, "So what's the problem now?"

If there is a problem, a twitching light bulb, a clogged drain, Frankie fixes it herself. No landlord. No phone calls. No foolery. When we shared a car and it snowed three feet, Frankie hurled a shovel under the buried tires, snowflakes like confetti in her hair.

"I think we're stuck," I shouted, watching her with a frozen face, hands in my coat pockets as the relentless wind bitch-slapped my cheeks.

"We're not," she said automatically. "Grab a shovel."

My phone buzzes on the coffee table and I ignore it. I know it's Andrew. Just like I suspected he pocketed our fortunes for a scrapbook. This is what Frankie would die for now, some guy to pose with in pictures, their arms linked like pretzels.

Frankie reaches over for my phone, her lips slightly parted.

"Oh shit," she says. "He's outside?" She tosses the phone in my lap, a bomb built just for me. She scrambles across the linoleum in her sweatpants.

"I think that's him in that car," she says. She's got her back against the wall, looking out the window like a secret agent. I brace myself against Andrew's text: *come outside!*

"What does he want?"

"Everything," I say. I go to my room to put on a pair of jeans, a Pats jersey, and my huge-ass gold hoops.

"Serena, wait," she says. She comes in with her Guess perfume, then dabs at my neck.

"That's good, that's enough," I say. "Am I high?" I ask Frankie, holding on to her forearms. Frankie frowns and genuinely thinks about this. A few minutes ago, we had made elaborate plans to be productive, but I forget what the plans were exactly.

"No," she says. "I'm high."

"Okay," I say, swimming in Frankie's eye contact. "I'll be back." She cups my cheeks with her palms.

"Go," she says, channeling her mom's Boston accent, "you whore." I smile at her, all the way like she's checking my teeth.

"Be good," she singsongs. I put my hand on the knob as she *shlacks* the lock. She makes a point of it. Perhaps I don't think to lock up because more days than not I wouldn't mind if one of those dopeheads walked on in and shot me, my face pooled in a salad-sized bowl of Cinnamon Toast Crunch.

"Hey," I say, bending down to the car where Andrew rolled the window. "You have a car?"

I wrap my arms around my chest, hugging someone. He cocks his head and laughs. Andrew has long, straight teeth, like a dentist's son. His hair really is blond, which disgusts me. I normally go for guys who are so dark they're mistaken for terrorists. Making old ladies scowl with their arms around my waist on the T.

"I rented it," he says meaningfully.

"It's Sunday," I say slowly, with equal meaning.

"You look like a rapper's girlfriend," Andrew says with that wide smile.

"Thank you," I say, moving my eyes over the vehicle, his palm balanced over the wheel, the vacuumed upholstery and spotless back seat. It smells new and sick, like sniffing glue.

"So, Miss Serena, can I take you somewhere?" he says.

*I don't know*, I think. *Can you?*

Maybe part of my disappointment lies in the fact that we didn't meet at the bar holding cold, wet umbrellas, seven shots deep with the stall locked, or online, talking dirty, back and forth, a prolonged handshake in the waiting room, he, my doctor, I, his patient, suddenly braless in his apartment, or at his office, so his wife wouldn't find out.

We met at the goddamn park. Frankie and I were on the swings, forcing our feet into the sky. We swung to the brink, then leapt off, our bodies like action figures against the fierce heat of the sun, fake crossing ourselves in midair.

He was walking his two-month-old puppy.

"Hi, puppy," Frankie said, crawling across the playground with wood chips stuck in her palms. "Can we hold him?" she begged.

He bent down, making a crease in his khakis as he released the leash. He grinned as he watched the dog scramble into Frankie's arms, where it pawed her shoulders, extending its tender belly to lick up her neck like ice cream.

Andrew sat on Frankie's swing. We watched her laugh, coo, then play dead as her hair sprawled over the wood chips and the puppy struggled across her legs. I made figure eights with my shoe, my grip infant-tight around the chains.

"I'm Andrew," he said, his nod as determined as a Hitler youth, his eyelashes faint in the sun.

"I don't want to hold the puppy," I said.

In the rental car, he leans over the passenger seat and swings open the door.

"Get in," he says, faking danger like in a rom-com. The wind blows my hair forward for a second. I feel Frankie's eyes on my shoulder from the sliver of the curtain.

We drive down Beacon Street, past the CVS where I sort of work, and where Frankie and I would be roaming aisles, trying on lipsticks if it weren't for this. We zoom past the bars we don't go to anymore because Frankie says they're infested with college kids, even though we're college kids.

"I don't know about you," he says as he makes a left turn towards the highway, "but I've been dying to get out of the city." The Citgo sign sinks, then disappears completely as we go down through the snake-cage flicker of the underpass.

We're now on I-93. Maybe I'm still high, but I have to admit, Andrew's kind of a good driver. He zips in and out of lanes, weaving through vans and four-wheelers with precision. His eyes move from the road to the rearview to me in a narcotized triangle. In my chest is a single tire, asphalt-hot, thwacking forward in a low hum.

But then he turns the radio up and starts drumming the wheel with his thumb, mouthing lyrics to this country song about living like you're dying. So here I am, trapped in a car with the kind of guy who would slowly then aggressively start singing "Bye, Bye, Miss American Pie" in unison with a bar full of strangers, fists and flipped stools punching the air over their heads. I check him again out of the corner of my eye. He rests his arm around my seat.

I don't want to know where we're going. This highway looks like every highway in America, though I've never been out of Massachusetts. The truth is I've driven down this highway my whole life. Once a month after my parents broke up, my brothers and I driving down I-93, Mom asking us deliberate questions like, "What in God's name do you eat at Dad's?"

I've told Frankie: When I was nine, my dad moved out of Boston to a rental house by a lake in Gloucester. He had a friend, Sharkey the manager, who would babysit us when my dad was gone. Sharkey had curly hair, the kind that looked wet, and a souped-up motorcycle he would carry me to, on the Fourth of July or after a couple beers. My brothers begged him to let them ride, but Sharkey only chose me, and he drove like dying was the aim, the helmet too big on my head. We zoomed down back roads, slicing free out of the still air. He'd lean to turn, my arms tightening on his waist. I thought of dropping from a plane. The glimpse into endlessness gave my laughter a screaming sound. And the engine burned my shins. The white outlines took on the vertical shapes of crocodiles, poised to belly forward.

After, Sharkey would watch us swim in the lake, that skin on my shins peeling a ghostly white. He hung our bathing suits on the shower rod and dried me off with my dad's thin towels, taking my legs up on the tub one by one. We watched VHS tapes on the armchair: *Problem Child, Coming to America.* My hair dried in crimps as Sharkey fell asleep behind me. Sometimes I still feel like I'm in the car while my parents scream in the driveway. My mom had seen the burns on my shins.

"Never again. Never again!" went her raging chant.

But I also used to drive down this highway with Frankie, on the first day Sonic opened or to the mall to buy summer dresses or sometimes just to drive, Frankie blazing up the bowl in a swirl with her knee on the wheel, blowing earrings of smoke rings, with my bare feet up on the dash, sunglasses down to turn the world a purple-black, and blabbing on about how bad we needed boyfriends even though I never felt lonely, then.

I let out a sigh and Andrew looks over at me. He's sporting puppy eyes, yearning for approval, or, worse, something I can't articulate. I push the window down a crack, but the air makes a screaming sound, so I seal it back up.

"I've never been out of Massachusetts," I admit.

"Really?" he says.

"Would I lie?" I say.

"You're mysterious."

"You're the one in a rental car," I say, "driving eighty-five miles an hour towards some town no one goes to so you can, what, dispose of my body in a polluted reservoir?"

We've been driving for an hour now. The trees that line the road grow as thick as our silence. My high's fading fast and I wonder what Frankie's doing. I text her: *I need you like my morning cigarette.* I cross then uncross my legs, watch how the clouds pretend to be faces. A monster opening its jaw, crazy gray smoke for eyeholes. I hear a lighter clicking, then Frankie's hysterical laughter, a laugh like a glass building shattering.

If I were home right now, in our kitchen with the Christmas lights, we might be taking everything out of the fridge and arranging it on the coffee table like a feast. The sun would creep across the hardwood as we'd lay crisscross on the couch, knifing peanut butter onto Oreos, towels twisted tight around our heads. Our faces would be caked in homemade sugar masks, the honey dripping slowly down our necks.

We'd be watching some forgotten movie like *L.A. Confidential* or *Uncle Buck* and then, when there was nothing else, repeats of *America's Next Top Model.* A commercial for a learning center would come on, an Asian woman with blushed cheeks speaking delicately into the camera as she waved a palm across the facility: "Here at Sylvan, we have a different approach to learning. . . ."

"We don't *learn*," I'd say, "but we *approach* it."

Frankie would laugh so hard she'd knock over my water, our fingers Cheeto orange and our bare feet pressed together in a contract.

"What the hell," I say as we pass a sign that reads, Welcome to New Hampshire. I turn back, gripping the headrest. "We're in New Hampshire," I say stupidly.

At the gas station, Andrew unbuckles carefully, the belt zooming across his chest. I think of all the things you can do in New Hampshire that you can't in Boston: wear flannel earnestly, drive trucks with Republican bumper stickers, carry guns. I flip down the visor and pat my lips with cherry ChapStick, then watch him from the side mirror as gasoline drips steadily from the pump in his hand.

He runs his fingers through his hair and it falls back across his eyes in pieces.

I'm thinking, *Every veterinarian has a freezer.* I'm thinking, *I'm being kidnapped,* and whatever it is that gets me to seeing him in a muscle tee, tattoos of dead relatives peeking out of the sleeve. There I am, tied to the Motel 6 bed, collarbones making a cavity in my neck as I suck in my breath.

"Shut the fuck up," he'd say as he cocked his gun. "And do what I say," he'd whisper, running his dick over my chapped lips.

I bite my nails as we pull out. He jams a CD into the player.

"I used to really like this band Bright Eyes in high school," he says. Conor Oberst whines as we drive.

I say, "He sounds like Doug Funnie but more suicidal."

I guess Frankie and I went through a Bright Eyes phase in high school. We did everything. Made out in front of guys, dressed as JonBenét Ramsey for Halloween, gave ourselves loopy tattoos with India ink, laxatives, arrests. With the India ink, we carved "+/−" into the blue of our wrists because Frankie said we're like batteries, keep each other balanced, charged. She'd lay out wet trash bags on strangers' roofs to tan, squeeze lemon juice over my head, pluck peach fuzz from my tummy trail, tilt my chin up in the girls' room mirror, hold me still, slip a needle through my tongue.

But Frankie's got some kind of itch now. Once we graduate, Frankie says we have to get married. At some point, kids. *But when we get divorced and move back in together, what would we do with the kids?* I thought. We lived with Nat and Raffa, and now it's just us, four apartments together and only sometimes I'm worried we'll keep going like that, apartment to apartment, making figure eights around Boston with our boxes of clattering candles.

Frankie will come home with a kitten that will become a cat, and it'll die before we do. We'll bury it illegally in the backyard. We'll hold vigil candles, our dream catcher earrings drooping our thin earlobes, tatty blankets wrapped around our shoulders like Russian shawls. Frankie will cry, covering her eyes with her fingers, and I won't know what to say, like the day her mom died.

She'll slip a stubbed-out roach from her sweater pocket and we'll blaze up, medical marijuana now 'cause we're on disability. We'll pitch cold shovels into the hard dirt as it starts to snow. Our neighbors will swipe back the curtains and call our landlord, adding to their growing list of complaints.

Back in the car, I have to say New Hampshire is a postcard. It's scenic and lush as it slices by in my window.

"Okay," Andrew says. "If you could go anywhere in the world—anywhere—where would you go?"

Return of the talk show host. Two can play. I steeple my fingers, then bend back my elbows, but it's my voice that cracks, "Do you believe in God or is the lack of God your God? If you were stranded on a deserted island, what is the one thing you would never bring? You ever get a girl pregnant?"

"You're real weird," he says.

"Case dismissed."

"We're almost there," he says, ticking on the blinker and pulling onto a two-lane highway past all the fast-food signage that glows over the whole road: *Get your six inches! Hot 'n' juicy. Try our new fish bites box.*

He parks in a bend in the middle of nowhere. Evergreens reach tall. Power lines rustle with an electric tinge like before it starts to rain, and I hope it does. The rain gets me.

"Follow me," he says.

We walk up a steep path, snap back branches, and climb up through the trees. We walk forever, falling into a hypnotic, fairy-tale pace, deeper and darker into the woods. The dirt dusts up my shins and sticks in the heat like the skin on a peach. I get thirsty but follow. The back of his neck gleams with sweat.

I once had sex with a stranger in woods kind of like this. We met at a bar and got drunk on PBRs. I whispered, "Let's go," my tongue flicking his ear after he spun me around on a barstool, faster and faster, my head thrown back like an over-sugared child. I woke up parched in my then-boyfriend's bed the next morning. I went to pee and found tiny, incriminating twigs in my hair and in my underwear.

"Are we almost there?" I ask.

We're both panting when we stop at an opening in the trees. He lifts me up by the waist. We climb onto this rock that ledges out before the drop, so high up it's like the end of a Jeep commercial. The sky as open as the washed-up wetland below.

"What is this?" I say. "The Grand Canyon of New Hampshire?" I tuck my hands inside my sweatshirt cuffs to hide my smile.

"It's called Deer Leap."

We sit at the edge on the weathered granite with our feet kicked off the ledge. From this angle, September comes on thick, the way the heat fades off the grass. But what now?

"This whole thing used to be a pond," he says, pointing to the deserted valley. "It dried up."

"Weird view," I say, the expanse of dead earth gaping under us, "for a voyeur."

I look up, trying to grasp something enormous, or alive. I want to be this girl who's taken with the sky, and sometimes I am, so I pull my hoodie up over my head and we kiss.

"You know what I like about you?" he says, taking my chin. I want to slither away, back under the leaves we marched on. "You're honest."

I pick up a pebble and squeeze it as hard as I can, chuck it as far as I can throw.

"Want me to be honest?" I say.

"Of course," he says, shaking my shoulder.

"Your puppy needs a bath. He smells like Doritos." I pick up another pebble, then steal a glance his way. He's recovering from the slap, nodding along and smiling too hard.

"More like Smartfood?" he says, his eyes narrowing.

"Can I be actually honest?" I say.

"I don't know now," he says, tearing open a pack of nuts from his backpack.

Frankie knows that the first time I masturbated I was nine. In my neighborhood, the kids played after school on this trampoline in my neighbor's backyard. After I did it, I lay in my bed, holding my hand over my chest to keep my heart inside my body. I could hear the kids shrieking frantically like birds. I remember being seriously worried that they were laughing at me.

One summer I wore gloves to summer camp because I thought I had AIDS.

In high school, Frankie and I went to this rager with an indoor pool. We did mushy coke off the diving board with a senior we barely knew who fed us blueberry Stoli, his arms around us in the hot tub. The next thing I remember I was getting pulled out by the cops. I can still feel the heat on my cheek from the hood of the cop car in the driveway, dripping wet, shivering in Frankie's bikini. A flashlight clicked and she was already in the back of the car.

The cop had my wrists locked, and I steeled my lower back against his crotch as he bent down to my ear and said, "Have you ever been arrested?"

I tried to pry my arms free and screamed, "Have you ever been raped?"

What if I told Andrew about Sharkey? How he lifted us up out of the armchair and laid me on my dad's springy mattress, where I waited, stiff as a knife. How he slipped his middle finger inside me like he was separating me from myself. How he laid that same hand on my chest, waiting for my breath, like on a doctor's table.

"Are you asleep?" he would say.

"Yes."

Frankie never had a dad, but she understands how the thought of him walking through the door at any second could make you come. I have dreams about Sharkey. We're in the supermarket, embarrassing everyone in the checkout. Underwater, can't tell that we're kissing, our throats filling up with bubbles. In the waiting room, he comes out in a white coat. The supermarket, the kissing, the white coat, night after night. In the white coat, he looks desperate. He's rushing to me, coming to tell me something critical, but it always stops right there.

Andrew has his arm around my waist as the sun drops fast. He's stroking the skin above my jeans, and I let him pull my shirt up.

"What does this mean?" he says.

He's thumbing the DNR tattoo on my rib cage. The most painful place for ink. I look at him, then burst into flames, laughing so hard that I'm afraid I'm going to pee. Andrew watches me, amazed. Frankie says my eyes sparkle when I laugh and that it's evil and contagious. No one knows me like she does. I swipe up the leaves, tear them to pieces, toss them into the abyss. I fall onto my side to catch my breath. Andrew lies next to me, our noses touching, that same, stupid-ass amazement in his eyes. I blink slowly so he can notice mine when they open, and say this instead: "I love you."

We say it the whole ride home. Him kissing the inside of my wrist with one hand on the wheel, at the toll, grinning at each other dopily while we wait for change, cars honking behind us, at the diner we stop at, the taste of grape jelly on my tongue.

"Can I call you tomorrow?" he says, the car idling outside my apartment. It's midnight.

"This was great," I say. "But can you unlock this?"

I bend down to the window because I need a place to lean. Any light between us flickers restlessly like last call. I walk away, knowing what I am. Free as the day God made me, but where's that guy been?

I climb into Frankie's bed, where she's buried, block Andrew's number, then cling to her pillow, caffeinated from the diner. Awake until it's light, the birds making frenzied, electronic chirps outside her window.

Later, Frankie's at her vanity, curling her hair for class. She looks at me in the mirror, our eyes catching. The rosacea on her cheek makes a flustered arc. I lie at the foot of her bed while she twists her hair around the iron. The room swells with the mist of her hair spray, thick lacquer like the rooms of a new house.

"Francesca," I say, "we should drive somewhere. It's not that hard to rent a car and move to LA."

In the corner of the mirror, Frankie's blush halves. She pulls the curler away, a section of her thick hair bouncing all tame up by her shoulder. I close my eyes and let the spray cover me from head to toe.

"We could become actresses or something," I say. "No one would even know us." I hear her lifting her backpack. Zipping her new boots.

"Hang on," I want to tell her. "I need you like a Tylenol PM."

Or something more: "I'd carve your name into my arm."

"I'm a fucking evangelist for your love."

I press the +/− on my wrist like a button on an elevator that won't stop dropping.

*Frankie, you're the positive. I'm the negative, aren't I?*

I feel my own tears begin to roll in the wrong direction, behind my ears and down the back of my neck and onto Frankie's sheets. And then her palm on my forehead like she's checking my temp. She moves it to my neck, where my pulse jumps, wet and receptive. She takes her hand away, then backs up to the door. I whisper, "You should skip class. Please?"

"I can't," she says.

She says, "Stop being sad."

I say, "I can't."

My eyes are still closed, but I can feel her there. The smallest creak, the *shlack* of the lock, the keys on her carabiner jangling off her hip as she skips down the steps. Why does she do this to me? I want to rip open the window and scream at the birds. I want Frankie to rip open the window to scream at me, just so I can scream back: "I'm not sad. Stay the fuck out of my business. Get your own life if that's what you want so bad. You think some guy is going to strong-arm you out of the muck? Good luck with it." But I stay still and stiff, my cold palm on my chest. I listen to my own heart beating two skips too fast.

Hear it? *Frankie. Frankie.*

# SHE SAYS SHE WANTS
# ONE THING

EVERYTHING I BROUGHT TO court was intentional, including the book. But when I looked down at my shoes, I noticed I'd forgotten to shave my legs, a mistake. The public prosecutor strode towards me in her pants suit. She circled my name on her clipboard. I felt chosen. She led the way to the conference room, which looked like a DJ's booth, that strip of thick glass. Inside it was just an office. I rested the book in my lap, as well as a pen I'd retrieved from my bun. The prosecutor was a woman, of course. I wrote down: *eye shadow, sooty like the rim of a Yankee Candle.*

"I have a quick question," I said, smiling my best smile, the one I used on my students when I allowed them to hand in work six weeks late. "I was wondering how long this will take. I may have to cancel an important meeting."

"Shouldn't be long," she said, then went on with it.

"Do you fear for your safety?" she asked. "Do you wish to press charges against Niko Vitalis?"

I went into autopilot. I'd pictured her more like a female James Lipton, but she was rushed and formulaic.

"Are you aware that dropping these charges will result in them disappearing forever?"

"Please turn off your phone," she said. Then I was led back into the row. Next to me was a girl my age deprived of eyelashes. She wore a tiny nose ring and an orthopedic boot on her foot—how obvious. The woman in front of us twisted in her seat and stared at me directly, her breasts flopping under a pilled blouse.

The men sat on the other side, leaning forward on the bench, rubbing together their palms. One of them stood, bending to run a belt through the loops on his sagging khakis. There was the young guy I saw outside the court, screaming into his girlfriend's face with a cigarette stuck to his lip. He looked belligerent, with the bloated red eyes of an alcoholic.

When I received the summons in the mail, I'd pictured just me and the judge as he read my case out loud, my understanding of the night in question deepening like a story narrated by a man with a serious voice. Then I pictured a cross-examination. Like an army kid in a new cafeteria, I could be anybody. Not anybody—different.

"Who is your favorite singer—alive or dead?" the lawyer would say, possessed by his pen, his head bent as he turned on his heel.

"I'm an adult."

"Would you consider yourself an optimist or a pessimist?"

"Only an optimist could sit in this seat."

"What are you writing down?" he'd say before pausing, the points of our pens frozen as if eyeing each other.

"The things that take my attention."

"After you began crying, what happened?"

"I'll tell you what happened," I'd say. I'd speak, my voice so faint that the stenographer would lean forward in her seat, her heels rising from their burrows in the plush of the carpet. The judge would take off his glasses slowly. He'd think of me at lunch as he stared curiously into the depths of his chicken Caesar salad.

"All rise," said the judge, a woman.

I'd been in the front pages of the book, writing: the judge's gold-etched name on the stand, describing her hair color, mom-blond. My sentences were microscopic on those blank pages where nothing is dedicated to anyone, no epigraphs to anchor any context. A man was called to the stand.

"Good morning, Mr. Johnson," the judge said.

Mr. Johnson had violated a no-contact order, missed parenting and anger-management classes, and, to top it off, would be back in court for a felony.

"He *has* been given chance after chance, *but*...," the public defender said. His black hair was slicked back in an impossible wave. I could see him sliding credit cards to waiters and the muscles that tightened his suit. He looked like an Armenian on a reality show, the kind of man whose sole purpose was to do the right thing by his family, no matter what.

*In God We Trust.* That was what was plastered on the wall, like an advertisement. I jotted it down, wrote: *Who is we?* The judge dismissed Mr. Johnson. And so it went. The women behind me in their printed blouses sighed as if we were waiting in line for another line. But the men on the other side were in worse shape. Violations, unpaid charges, subsequent offenses. The judge nodded to them each affably. She was stern but friendly as a kindergarten teacher, one from the Midwest, who bent to correct an unzipped fly or to hand you a fresh sheet of paper. I wrote it all down.

"Are you employed?" she asked the delinquent kid with the bloated eyes.

"Nah," he said. He had nicks on the back of his skull from a garage buzz. I could tell, even with his back turned, that he had his fists crossed in front of his crotch, as if to say, "Suck it."

I zoned out hard as I moved my pen across the page but jerked as the kid smacked open the gate with his palms. I heard him say something like, "Ah, fuck yeah," as he limped clean out the double doors, the gate swinging wildly behind him. The judge and the handsome defender shared a moment as they huffed, rolled their eyes. By this point I had slipped into the first row, and assumed they'd turn to me next. We would triangulate, shaking our heads, mystified with the idiocy of this delinquent moron.

Next up was a man I hadn't noticed who walked to face the judge like he was tiptoeing across an endless sheet of ice. He wore a light blue cotton shirt and matching pants like nurses' scrubs. He had his own attorney. The attorney had cotton ball hair like a Floridian. He stood erect as a surfboard in the sand, speaking to the judge in a loud, demanding tone that made both her and me turn our attention to him from opposite vantages.

"I'd just like to say"—his voice rebounded from the wooden walls—"for the record..."

Now, this attorney was the kind of man who could smack a woman and get away with it. He was building empires with his lies and spoke with force, so you'd be slow enough to agree. It took energy, for which I had none, to steel myself against agreeing. The man who the attorney was representing pounded at his chest—I was surprised a chicken bone didn't fly out—and shifted his feet from one side to the other.

" . . . that the plaintiff, who, might I add, has a *warrant*, has contacted me multiple times, though there is record that she has dropped the charges against the defendant. She calls me repeatedly. She showed up unannounced at my office. A stripper with a warrant . . ."

The judge looked down at the attorney patiently.

". . . I don't believe it!"

The man in handcuffs held his forearms over the table and leaned as though he were stretching for a marathon.

"She says she wants one thing, and then she does another. I mean, as you know, this is what happens with domestic violence cases."

"It's what *can* happen," the judge corrected. "Sir, are you okay?"

"He has Crohn's disease," the attorney spat, like she was a fucking idiot and always would be for not knowing.

"He can be excused," she said, and the sheriff held her hand over his back to guide him through the back door as he hobbled.

I could have sat there all day. I was sleepy enough anyway, my name creeping up on the list. More cases. More cases. Everything moving through the tight screen of logistics. Yes or no. How many months. Amount of the bail. Why were we women rowed up on the benches audition-style when we were the ones who deserved to leave first? The room was split in two, and these slum, criminal wife-beaters were getting to go first, while the ring-twisting women they had beaten and would beat again had to wait for hours, listening to the litany of their charges, wasting entire days of their lives.

My life specifically. I was dead-ending at an after-school program in Dorchester, managing teenagers who talked over me on a good day. I was supposed to go for a run, maybe even reread the book on my thigh. There should have been a suggestion box outside the courtroom. The men received all the attention, so much emphasis on their situations, whereas when we women were finally called to the stand, one by one, we were asked, one hand raised to God, if we'd like to proceed with the case we had initiated. And then we were dismissed. Not a woman proceeded.

I wrote down every observation in the courtroom that day while I waited four more hours. I was writing a story, and needed to remember all the details. The judge's bench where something like a McIntosh apple should have been sitting shiny, the belt clicking against the man's starved waist, the eye shadow like candle smoke, raised hands. In God We Trust.

"Do you trust in God?" I pictured the lawyer asking me.

"I'm no client," I'd say.

At one point a large woman in a do-rag opened the gate and dragged her tiny son behind her. The boy looked drawn from a picture book and dropped his hand from her grip, then reached up to slip a phone the size of his head out from her back pocket. He moved his fingers over the shattered screen as the woman held up her palm. The phone sounded through the room, the disrupting jangle of an ice-cream truck.

"Shhhhhh," she hissed as she reached back for his collar.

"It's okay," the judge said. "It's all right."

When I couldn't write anymore, I pictured myself rising above the women. Had the judge noticed me sitting there, writing, or would she notice me when I walked through the gate, my face unwrinkled, my cheekbones high like a child's, mighty? I would walk to the stand, puncturing the disaffected haze of their side. My hair twisted back in a way that looked trustworthy and refined. I'd hold the book in my hands.

After this, there'd be two months of happiness. Real happiness, not the kind you have to lie about. And then Niko would call me one day after I spent money at Target on jeans and a comforter. He'd call it his money and why this and why that. Guess what. It was his money. He'd push me up the stairs—yeah, up, because I was moving too slowly. He'd hit me so hard across the nose with a dress shoe that my own blood would shoot across the dining room and cover the glass hutch, where I kept books instead of dinner plates. I'd hold my nose as I fell, the cartilage blown to rubber. Permanently, it would look like the manic swerve of a tire track.

"You're too pretty to be here," the judge would say. Or, softly, "What is that you're reading? Come."

I would hold up the book, place it in her hands. She would turn it over, read each starred review. Make the connection. At night, her husband would try to kiss her on the cheek as she tucked her hands under a pillow, her eyes open to a dark wall. She would do nothing but dream of me. I was that bright. I pictured it exactly like this, as one of the best days of my life.

# FRANKIE

# CRIBS

## SUMMIT AVE

Raffa comes to live with you in December during school break.

You and Natalya have a two-bedroom off Harvard Ave, a quiet street. You've gotten used to Nat's half-hung Freddie Mercury posters and dirty laundry, splitting toilet paper but not toothpaste. You haven't gotten used to Nat's hushed green eyes, her bee-stung lips, a beauty so rough that it's pretty.

You and Nat have never been in one fight. At night, she plays you Paolo Nutini from her laptop. She lets you read her father's love letters from Ukraine.

You and Nat carry Raffa's new Ikea bed up through the snow, heavy on the black ice of the stairs. Nat looks at you like Raffa's draped across it. The three of you crack Budweisers as Raffa folds jeans into a dresser she sticks in the front hall, holding pairs up by your hips, tossing them to you for trying on. Raffa wants to paint the kitchen electric purple and buy a fruit basket. Nat guzzles her beer too fast and it gushes out her nose like a science project. The neighbors next door have kids and knock softly, asking you to please keep it down.

In the living room, you push the couches into one bed and fall asleep at 3 a.m., for months. Raffa doesn't step away to take phone calls and talks loudly in her sleep. Every cabinet is crammed. Every wall is covered. At Summit, there is less and more space.

## THE HILL

Everybody gets fat in one day. You are ravenous and rarely full. Raffa's friends from school come to your place on Griggs Street, and your kitchen is always bumbling. You run out, like gypsies across the train tracks on Comm Ave, in peasant skirts with your hair tied up at the top.

At 7-Eleven you infiltrate aisles, cackling by the freezer. You line up to dump Doritos, ramen noodles, Boston cream doughnuts in cellophane baggies, sunflower seeds, Mini-Wheats, and a gallon of milk onto the counter in front of Manny, who watches you shop from the surveillance with a toothpick in his teeth. Serena always needs two more dollars, so you fish for quarters at the bottom of your backpack, careful not to look up at Manny.

Serena slips through your cracked bathroom window when your keys drop through the gutter's steaming bars. She makes a mess of mac and cheese and passes around the pot. Doughnuts with bite marks sit in the flower-painted fruit bowl on top of last year's Halloween candy and packets of matches from bars you've never been to.

She moves in wordlessly, falls asleep in your bed, head to foot. She wakes up laughing from bad dreams. Her hair dyed and dark at the roots. She buys the shampoo, the Kool-Aid, the nail polish, the Tylenol PM. Leaves it in the medicine cabinet, fills empty Advil bottles with dental meds.

On the toilet, you let Serena comb her fingers through your hair. She mixes up a box of clearance Nice'n Easy and smooths out tinfoil, her wifebeater cutting above her hips. Your eyes level with her belly button, a surprised mouth. Nat leans against the doorway, snaps her Nikon. You don't care when your hair fries to wisps and Serena cuts it, or how big you are. You will all lose weight by the fall. In the apartment, there is more and less of you.

# LORRAINE TERRACE

You finally move to a place with a porch behind an elementary school and it's like a clubhouse. Raffa's leaving to go abroad in a month, and just in time, her ex-boyfriend Mickey gets her pregnant. She stays inside all month like a house cat you can only pet or observe. She stays by the sink, rinsing bowls. On your new porch, painting her nails intently, listening for the soundtrack of a distant recess. She rests, facing the wall in her Ikea bed, which starts to look like a wrought iron crib.

After her abortion, it barely becomes spring. You go out to the porch. It's wet from icicles dripping fast and smells like cardboard rushing down a river. Inside you had scrawled wishes onto torn sheets of notebook paper. Nat throws a match into a red bucket, then follows the smoke with her lens.

Seconds become days become summer. The apartment makes you itchy. The summer's superstitious. Curtains billow like ghostly skirts. Raffa's flicking her perpetual cigarette. She tells you the nurse who gave her an ultrasound traced the screen with her finger and said, "Twins."

# ELIOT STREET

In Allston, you hear they call September first Christmas, and now you know why. You sit on a collapsing box, surveying all the mismatched dining room chairs you found on the curb, airing your stomach out with your T-shirt.

"It's hotter than outside," Nat says, her cheeks a secret pink.

"Guys, get in," Raffa says from the bathroom, where she's running water.

You sit on the edge as Nat and Raffa and Serena undress. The water sways slowly like it knows something. They dip their toes, then lower themselves in. Raffa stops the drain, her spirals half soaked down her shoulders. She lights a cigarette.

Next year, you and Serena will move into your own place on Berkeley Street, the cathedral's bells an alarm clock. The clouds passing fast as screen savers outside your window behind the still, torn faces of the billboard's women. Nat will move to San Francisco for a job in advertising. Raffa will move to the North End with Mick. You'll talk on the phone.

"When we have kids," Raffa says, dangling her wrist, "you'll be aunties."

She places the cigarette in Nat's lips. Nat extends her neck to exhale, blowing smoke away from you. You skim your fingers across the water as ash falls to the surface and separates, blackening to bits of lace.

"And when we get divorced," Raffa finishes, "we'll all move back in."

You smile. She winks. You're waiting, for this heat to let up, for fall to bleed out into winter. For now, you are pool balls, in your triangular lifetime, waiting to get shot out and whirled.

# STAGE FOUR

**WHAT I DID WAS** held my hand out like a gun and sprayed. I was supposed to be wiping down tables. But there was something about walking through the pink mist—I can't tell you the feeling. That clinical smell that clung to my neck like antiseptic perfume. At that time and that time only, I liked doing the opposite of what I was told.

I was breathing in the rinsed air when this guy wandered in and crouched down at the end of the bar. He was in a white blouse with one of those dog-chain gang-rape necklaces gleaming down his neck. I watched him, a bold move that made him turn to me as he tapped his combat boot on the leg of the stool.

"What are you doing?" he said. I set the cleaner down.

"What are you wearing?" I came back with. I contemplated his soft-spoken British accent, his inflection so authentic I thought I could hear it in a voice-over. He just sat there looking like someone from the past, like Steven Tyler, the pouty-lipped version from my mom's broken, old records. I started wiping beer puddles with a stiff rag across the laminate, afraid I might actually get in trouble this time.

"Tell me, who's in charge here?" the guy said.

I glanced at my boss, the manager of Bukowski Tavern, this nice kid named

Larry who sat on a barstool by the door. Not to check IDs but strictly just to stare out the window like a lapdog. His hair was going prematurely wispy. He kept one leg on the floor with the visible outline of his penis through his gray sweatpants. I grimaced.

"That would be me," I said, making my way behind the bar.

"Young lady," he said secretively, bending forward like we were on the surveillance. "Care to route an old-fashioned my way?"

He tipped back on the stool so his ladies' blouse slid up, and for a second I wished he would tip all the way back, get embarrassed, then scatter out of my bar.

"Who are those for?" he asked. He pointed to the tiny pairs of stockings hanging from the top liquor shelf, the Christmas decorations Larry hadn't bothered taking down. The stockings were ice skates, bowed and pink. He wanted me embarrassed.

"They're for Nancy Kerrigan," I said.

He had no idea what I was talking about, so I just ignored him, wet the sugar, then crushed and stirred the way Larry taught me on my first day, when I handed him a W-2 and my fake ID. I turned back briskly for a touch of drama, held up a crinkled plastic bottle of soda water. I let it fizz to the top till I felt him looking at me, deep, like it didn't occur to him that a stare like that could hurt me. A stare that recognized how bad I was at pretending. I screwed the cap back on and kept my eyes low.

"Emma Chizit," he said.

"Who?" I said.

"Ow, much, is it?" he said.

When I smiled, he said, "Are you having a laugh?" and I nodded, noticing the rice pilaf coloration of his front teeth.

I said, "Ten bucks," rounding up because I could. When he looked at me sideways, fishing through his pockets, I said, "Cheers," and reminded myself of the tube-topped waitresses I saw in movies when I was a kid at sleepovers. Girls who leaned in and winked at their regulars like plastered ads on billboards. Those nights I'd miss my mom so much that I'd lay awake on a trundle bed convinced she was getting hit by a car, or the one hitting—right that second—though it was two in the morning and I knew she was home, asleep on the couch with the light from the TV pouring over the bottles of Carlo Rossi on the coffee table. The QVC ladies sweeping mops across the floor, their mouths moving on mute, though I wished she would hear: *This broom will change your life, I guarantee it.*

"I just returned from this festival called Pitchfork," the guy said. "Have you heard?"

"No," I said. I leaned my palms against the bar and stretched my calves. The balls of my heels going up and down as I thought of how many calories I could be burning. He tapped his dirt-etched fingers on the bar, then ran them through his hair. It was long and coarse with streaks of gray running through.

"What's your name?" I asked.

"Villy," he said, twirling a toothpick between his fingers.

"Billy?" I said.

"No. But I like the way you think," he said. "Will you come with me?"

He wiped his lip with a silky sleeve, then turned out his palm. I looked at Larry with his eyes closed and his arms crossed and his mouth open to the point of almost fogging the window, and after a few seconds I heard this other girl inside me say, "Sure."

After we ducked into a cab and Villy called out, "To the races!" and the Pakistani cab driver shook his head, spat out the window, then shot into traffic, Larry called me eight times and left three voice mails, one asking if I was in the restroom, the second to update me on the fact that he had checked the restroom and that there was shit in the toilet, which was also technically my job to clean, and the third to tell me to come the fuck back to work or he'd fire me and he really didn't want to do that. I told you he was nice. We left the cab after Villy tossed some fives towards the dashboard.

"This way," he said, and we cruised through the automatic doors at the Prudential. We took the elevator up all the way to the fifty-second floor, and when we got to Top of the Hub, he kissed me. A man in a black bowtie played a cello in the corner, his arm dipping to scrape the strings, his torso convulsing theatrically. Villy and I were in each other's eyes, every look a dare, and the waiters who darted around us felt far as planets. But then the hostess glanced at my lower half. I was in torn jeans and a black apron. I thought to crawl to the table. Beyond the blue reflective glass, the buildings sat below us like a village of batteries. Villy took his time with the wine list as sweat fell between my boobs in the lines a necklace makes.

Outside, smiling as I accidentally burped, the taste of grape juice in the air, Villy lifted me up so our noses touched in one long goodbye. His hair smelled like smoke, when you tear off the filter. Instead of pulling a penny from my ear, he slid a pair of sunglasses from his sleeve, then perched them on my ears. "Ray Charles," he said. "I wish you luck getting home."

Boston is small, meaning you can go far without actually going far, so I walked the fuck back to work after I blindly wrote my number on Villy's forearm with a green permanent marker he'd extracted from his coat pocket along with a packet of ketchup, which he also let me keep.

Villy and I started going on dates—strictly at hotels with names like Alibi or the Envoy. It was like something I didn't order but came in the mail anyway, Villy: a man, one who sniffed wine before sipping, who thought the New England Patriots were colonists, not the spandex-wearing beef-balls on the flat-screen at my bar. Plus, his name stuck to the tip of my tongue so I could say it in my mind over and over until it crashed into itself: *Villy Villy Vilililily.*

He wore fitted wallpaper suits and brown and green braided bracelets that I assumed some topless woman tied to his wrists at Pitchfork. I wore Serena's black dress, the one she kept on the floor of her closet after her father's wedding, and each time a different sweater in the hopes Villy wouldn't notice. If he did, he didn't let on, because one night, when I climbed into the cab outside my mom's house, he said, "You look positively smashing."

"And where are you going?" my mom asked before I dipped. She tapped her cigarette into a mug, the kiss of her orange lipstick stained on the brim.

"Does it matter?" I said.

I saw the cancer in her lungs like a seismic monitor, the red orbs blinking across the length of her chest, then up her throat, curling out her lips like contagious neon smoke.

"You shouldn't smoke," I added.

"Does it matter?" she said, her throat so dry she began to cough like a barking seal. I took advantage and slipped out the front door.

On our third date, Villy cued the waitress and she bent down to his lips as he cocked his head back to her ear, the sharp line of his jaw moving up and down just slightly. It was the first time I can remember feeling jealous, like this creamy-skinned waitress was jotting her pen directly onto my heart, carving something intricate and critical there that I would never be able to see. Villy was pointing to the dimly lit calligraphy, one leg crossed over the other, his arms hanging loose on either side of the upholstered chair as her blond hair hung like a fancy curtain around his head.

"Fantastic!" he said as she tucked the menu back under her arm. He'd ordered vinegar fries with aioli that swirled at the top and I was impressed, though later I learned the sauce is just mayonnaise that went to college.

The drinks between us were twirling pink and bubbling as he stared at me for melodramatic pauses like a psychologist. I wanted to mimic his pose, challenge his own notion of himself back, but under his gaze I felt like a broken toll—anything could pass through me. Satisfied with my blankness, he'd lurch forward to take my hands.

"You're blushing," he said.

"It's rosacea."

"I used to be the creative director at an ad agency when I lived in London," he said. "Before that, an intellectual property lawyer."

I squinted as I chewed my straw. I couldn't picture either, but I liked all those words strung together, *property* and *intellectual*, *director* and *agency*. Also *lived*. When I lived somewhere. I hadn't lived anywhere but with my mom in our same split-level off the highway with the aboveground pool in the back, the whir of cars from Route 9 making coastal sounds through the rotting fence.

"My father was a plastic surgeon," he said. I think my face dropped, because he said, "Not like that. He's retired now. He performed rare and complex surgeries for children with cleft palates. Do you know what those are?"

"Children?" I said.

He loosened his jaw. "Fissures around the lips." He pointed.

"I've seen that," I said. "On commercials."

"So I lived in Nicaragua. My mum, she was a photographer for Italian *Vogue* but shot miniatures in her spare time." He lifted my hands from the table, and they dangled, pale and reflexive.

"She's going to love you," he said. "You have such Lilliputian wrists!"

Then he grew serious; he looked at me acutely as he held his drink to the side.

"They could be on display," he said, "at a museum."

I don't know why, it was the weirdest thing, but I started to cry.

Outside, we stood pressed together under a blue awning. Villy had his coat collar turned up, and it outlined his neck like a cape. His sideburns were dark and artificial looking. He marched ahead to wave down a cab, clasping his thumb and forefinger around my wrist like a bracelet. My heels scraped against the black ice, the wind slicing past my cheeks like welcome razor blades.

The first time I went back to Villy's apartment I stayed for four months straight. I only took the bus home once for a backpack to fill with clothes and makeup. It was just getting to be spring and the grass in my front lawn bent in frost-laced patches. My mom's sister's red Corolla was parked on the curb. I walked through the back, the porch I'd painted the past summer already chipping where the wood curved, two of the rails broken and damp from spring rain.

My aunt had sprayed Febreze to mask the sweet smell of vomit from the bathroom hallway. Her wooden clogs clunked across the floor of my mom's bedroom and echoed like trees falling in dreams. Outside the door, I listened as the sheets shifted. My mom's steady wheezing was that of an extraterrestrial.

My aunt hung on to the doorway of my bedroom as I hurled bras into a duffel bag. She had the laundry basket balanced on her hip and her glasses strung by beads down her neck. I despised how well she played nurse when my mom had been one for the better part of her life. Now her cough was breaking through the hallway.

When my aunt asked me if I was in school, I lied.

When she asked where I was going, I lied.

When she asked if I would call my mom when I got there, I told her the truth. I said, "No."

Villy said, "After you, little wing," and we stepped into his building for the first time in Dorchester, across the street from a Mobil station. The stairway was dark and smelled like Indian food and ash. I thought I could hear a baby crying from down the hall. Villy tossed his keys on the counter and flicked on a twitching kitchen light. I think he was nervous as I walked the length of his studio apartment, because he offered to make oysters Rockefeller. He also had bacon. I said that would be fine. He clicked on the stove.

I recognized the Kirkland-labeled dish soap and the flimsy look of discount furniture, the gleam of the screws on the outside of the bookshelf. Villy had tacked silky emerald-green sheets above the windows to resemble the inside of a nightclub. Bacon crackled in the stove like Pop Rocks, and Villy forked out strips, then set a plate down on the piano bench he kept in front of a red leather reclining chair. He uncorked a bottle of red wine and we clinked glasses.

"*Salut*," he said.

"What?" I said.

"Ha!" he said, tucking the hair behind my ears. "It's like I found you on *Star Search*."

We shared the sunken recliner, flipping through the channels on his tiny TV. I nibbled at the burnt bacon and he let me pick a rerun of *Sex and the City*, one of those early episodes where Carrie's hair is genius-crazy and she's always saying, "I got to thinking . . ."

It was the first time I felt like his girlfriend because he had his arm around my shoulders and kissed me right on my neck freckle every minute or two.

"You know," I said, looking at him, "I always thought I was a Charlotte, until that one episode where Miranda eats cake from the trash."

He let me finish the bottle of syrupy wine. I slurred something about loving him, then went to the bathroom to yak. Villy held my hair back. The toilet bowl looked like some reckless girl had her period.

"I'm sorry," I said, my voice echoing in the bowl.

"Oh, Ray, you've only spilled your drink."

By the end of that first week we had a routine. Every morning we would lie around listening to records and I would try not to think of my mom, what the doctor said about the dark blood that stained at the corners of her mouth as if she'd done her lipstick while turning off an exit on the highway. It was the hardest then because it was the only time it was bright in Villy's apartment and I could see things exactly as they were: toothpaste uncapped in the bathroom, the kitchen sink brimming with streaked glasses, the spill of sun on the twisted sheet, the scare of Villy's dyed hair peeking through.

It was the first few minutes of morning, when you look around and there's light everywhere, so much light you can see particles floating towards you as you blink, and you piece yourself together object by object: the toothpaste in that bathroom is mine, I drank from those glasses in the sink, the breathing man under the warm sheets is now speaking to me.

Villy liked to give me what he thought was a proper education, which mostly had to do with good wine and vinyl records. *Band of Gypsys* was second-best to *Are You Experienced*. *Bridges to Babylon* made the Rolling Stones sellouts. He banned the TV and liked to pace around as if he was standing in front of a chalkboard. I'd have on one of his button-ups as a dress, a hole stabbed in one of his old belts to make a tight notch, my knees clutched together on the side of the recliner. I'd go to work at night at Bukowski Tavern, then come back on the last bus to Villy's with a to-go bag of soggy french fries to split.

Each week that passed, I noticed something new and ridiculous about Villy that I hadn't before. His fashionably advanced garments started to look like discounted neon windbreakers on an Urban Outfitters rack.

One day, after he wiped down my back with a dress sock, he said, "I'd like to institute a new method to our lovemaking—condoms." He said this as I crouched in front of his antique floor-length mirror, looking at him looking somewhere far off, shirtless and gleaming like he'd just made a new rule as king.

Villy said he'd been laid off because of the economy, but instead of applying for jobs, he sat on the recliner with a pipe between his lips.

He said, "Ray, we need to mobilize resources."

This meant selling the recliner outside his building to a pregnant chick for twenty bucks. I helped her lift it onto the bus. When her T-shirt rose, the purple swell to her belly button looked like a black eye.

I lost my Boston accent but regained it when we fought. Sometimes six fights a day. I have to admit, the fighting was exciting. It made me feel proactive, like I was using some kind of gym membership, rhetorical kickboxing.

One day I made PB&J, and Villy said, "Ray, that's not the correct knife to spread the jam."

I pointed the knife at his chest. "Then what kind of knife is it?" I said through my teeth.

Villy looked down at me, his hair in all directions. "The jagoff bar you work at. What's it called again? Is it called Smart Little Bitch's?"

I'd bring him tea in bed and he'd look at me like I poisoned it. "Did you make this with the Boston water you grew up on? You're derailing my morning process."

"Strange," I said. "Last time I checked it was four o'clock."

"You need to be one hundred percent nicer," Villy said, whipping off the sheets.

"Do you want to go to lunch? Or dinner at this point. I'll pay," I offered.

"Every now and then," Villy said, cupping my face, "you say something worthy. Then we give you a lot of praise and we move on."

Instead of going to dinner, he opted to gift me with a joint-rolling lesson.

"Not a psychobabble amount, Ray. Roll it like a pinner."

"A what?

"A real toothpick of a joint."

"Jesus," I muttered. "I think I might not have graduated from the same finishing school."

I started to wonder—how could Villy be so poor and pretentious at the same time? Where was he getting money from, when he wasn't getting money from me? We had sixty-six bucks from my last paycheck at Bukowski Tavern. Larry had fired me a week earlier because Villy would walk in during my shifts just to sit at the end of the bar and stare at me.

"All right," Larry said finally, after Villy had flicked a maraschino cherry at my head and missed. "You're done."

Before I left for good, I had to wait at the end of the bar for twenty minutes till my french fries resurfaced in the fryolator.

"I already fucking ordered them!" I screamed from the other side of the window as Villy held his palms up outside, then paced the sidewalk with a cigarette perched on both ears. That was during the second month, month two, and I couldn't even look at Larry. Larry didn't look at me, either. He never had anyway.

But Villy found something out when he looked over my shoulder as I was depositing that last paycheck at the ATM. I had two thousand bucks sitting smack in my savings from a school loan before my mom got sick and I dropped out of community college. I'd skipped a grade and was young for a freshman, seventeen.

"Technically, it's not usable. It's not real money," I explained to Villy as we sat on his front steps watching the morning bus lurch by. "Because it's a loan and because I'm going to go back."

"Everything is real, Pilgrim," Villy said, tapping my forehead. "Do you know what solipsism means?"

He tried to tuck my hair behind my ear, but I blew smoke in his face.

"I'm not in college, so no," I said, "you asshole."

"Calling me names, Ray, is just another desperate plea for rules and consequences, of which you have none."

I obviously didn't know what solipsism meant or why anyone would use it in an actual argument, but I knew that my loan money was untouchable. Villy could not convince me otherwise. I pictured the discolored triangles of his teeth gleaming insanely as cash blew on the wind past his head. The money I'd left for my mom in the bread box when I was fifteen so the Jeep wouldn't get repossessed, all that money I'd saved so she could drink piss wine, and now she was truly sick and where was I? That money could be for her if I let myself think about it long enough, which I couldn't.

"Never mind. You were right. Nothing is real," he said. "Which is *why* you're not going back to school, Ray." He fingered my dangling handcuff earring, then flicked it.

"What are you talking about?" I said. He sighed as I palmed a tear from my cheek.

I became not allowed to answer the phone. Villy would leave and the phone would ring and I'd pick up.

"I told you not to answer the phone," Villy would say on the other end.

"Where in the living Christ of hell are you?"

"Meet me at that bar," he said, wildly out of breath as he promptly hung up.

*Let me consult my pride,* I'd think, *and get back to you.*

We fought about the phone and the not-real money and other things, on the cold concrete staircase as we stubbed out cigarettes like we were killing ants and his neighbors tiptoed over us, or at the late-night movie we snuck into, then got kicked out of for starting a screaming match during the previews as the mice darted through the aisles.

"Why do you swear so much, princess?" Villy whispered, the sick smell of butter on his breath.

"Because fuck you!"

One time I swore I saw him stealing shiny blocks of butter from the high-end grocery store he made us go to at least twice a week. He slipped three of them into his messenger bag, just one after the other like he was rescuing kittens. I glared at him while we stood in line, and when he peered into my basket, he raised his voice at me.

"Fuji apples?" he said. The checkout girl with the maroon vest and the name tag that read *Mandy* peeked up at us.

"I told you. Pink Lady." When I wouldn't look at him, he tapped out the syllables on my forehead. "Pink. La-dy," he repeated. "What are you, demented?"

I waited on the bench by the Coinstar while Villy went to the bathroom, probably to steal toilet paper, when checkout Mandy walked up to me. She had bangs that looked like they'd been blow-dried sometime in the early nineties and then preserved right like that on her forehead.

"Hi," she said, the bright zits on her jawline looking about as unsanitary as a salad bar. When I didn't respond, she said, "If you wanna job here or something, I can ask my manager."

She popped her gum, pink string stuck to her cheek like her tongue exploded exactly where I'd aimed.

"What are you, demented?" I said.

Her bottom lip dropped and started to twitch, which made mine twitch. I kind of wanted to hug her—I hadn't hugged anyone in a long time. Instead, I stormed off and waited for Villy in the parking lot, even though it was drizzling and the heavy brown bags were starting to tear from the bottom. I did need a job. It wasn't my idea to spend the last of our money on assorted cheese trays and grape-seed oil.

When we got home, I threw my headphones on and walked out of Villy's place as he yelled "Prima!" from the window. I crossed the highway where the strip mall sat with the Staples sign half lit. I walked all the way to Southie and sat back on one of those rusted-up swing sets by the beach, kicking my feet into the air. The cold was so hostile it made the clouds look as if their punishment were to hang there and watch.

In my headphones, I had the *Schindler's List* theme song blaring on repeat, the one with the trembling violin that sounds like it's weeping. I felt the bow scrape against my rib cage. My feet pumping and the soaring through the stinging air created the false sensation that I was moving forward. The swings were the one place where time fixed itself. I didn't want to admit that time had started to feel like a machine, a spaceship going the wrong way. Every moment I was moving back towards being entirely and completely my mother's.

I got dizzy and kicked to a stop. Also, a kid with a puffy jacket and snot running down his gleaming upper lip had been standing there pouting at me for more than fifteen minutes. Swing sets need more swings. I walked dumbly home to Villy's, amazed and numb by my own capacity for so much sadness. Behind the bars, by the dumpsters, I mistook a rat for a squirrel and didn't flinch. I was floating, trying not to think more about how the heart's a muscle like any other, one that memorizes its contractions.

Towards the very end, I started to see how strangers saw Villy—and this made me want to die in place of someone else. Instead, I hid myself in his coat just to leap out and startle them. Like the captain of the duck tour when Villy strode down the aisle and said, "Excuse me! Captain!" like we'd ordered a car service. "Captain, care to deliver us to Copley Center?"

"Read the map, chief."

Villy whipped the hair from his eyes as we tipped back, the driver making a wide, purposeful turn through the dark water. A lady looked up at me from her pamphlet, her lips pursed into the unmistakable shape of an asshole. Instead of asking what she was looking at, I waved my arm at the driver, then pointed at Villy and said, "Is your presupposition, chief, that this man is literate?"

I saw it, and I didn't. Villy made me tea and swirled it with a stick of honey. He came to where I faced the wall, curled up in his bed. The ceiling fan whirred as I pictured myself hanging from it. Villy and I were strangers who had collided with each other on the sidewalk, hard, and I was too tired to get up and walk away.

He slid me to him. He whispered, "Never, never, never leave me, Booger," turning my chin like a photographer angling my cheek to the correct light. I half smiled, the hook. He asked me to go get the mail downstairs, but not if it was bills. I did it, and I noticed the paper slips piling up outside his front door like pizza coupons. I knew he hadn't been paying rent. There were shades of stupidity that could be attractive to a girl like me. This wasn't one of them. That same day my mom called as I sat on the edge of the tub fully clothed with the door locked.

"Frankie," my mom said. I could barely hear her. Her voice was different for being exactly the same. "I need you to do something for me."

I reached back to turn up the water so I couldn't hear her, but she wouldn't shut up. I blamed the Dilaudid for slurring her speech, but I was sick of her calling me during blackouts. Demanding I fix things in a voice that was as empty as the tire on the Jeep when she crashed into the fence of a golf course.

What my mother said drunk, on a loop that hurt every time, were clear answers to questions I preferred to keep foggy.

"I hate my life!" she had cried as I pictured the Jeep steaming beside her. "My life is garbage."

Or when I came home late and she propped herself up to say, her pants wet with piss, "You are the last person I want to see."

"You are an embarrassment," I said. I hung up, a habit I can barely talk about.

I kept seeing Villy long after I left his apartment on a Tuesday, my toothbrush, bra, and deodorant tied in a plastic CVS bag. I waited stone-faced by the bus stop while Villy hung his head out the third-floor window and sang "Helpless" as he flicked a cigarette from a pack of American Spirits I'd left on the counter.

I slightly broke my composure and screamed, "Shut the hell up, you motherfucking fuck!"

"*And in my mind, I still need a place to go, all my changes were there,*" he crooned. I hurled my plastic bag up to the window, but it made a low arc, then dropped at my feet.

"Where are my oysters?" I screamed.

My cheeks were burnt with tears, but the one I was screaming at was myself. I'd caved. I'd taken out the rest of my school savings, the not-real money now really real, and paid two months' worth of Villy's rent. I felt like a kid who was being kept inside during summer vacation, which in a way I was. It was June and unusually hot, and everyone had their windows thrown open, which made Villy's strangely on-key serenade all the more humiliating.

In July, the week my mom died, I stayed with Villy for the actual last time. This I can tell you because it's all I remember: he took me to the Mobil station across the street, the farthest I could walk. I asked him to hide me in the long coat he wore despite the heat, and he did. We walked the aisles in stumbling stride, me shoeless in Villy's coat with my tiptoes on his dress shoes. He kept me wrapped up as he picked out Hostess cupcakes and ghost-shaped mac and cheese, along with twenty dollars' worth of Tylenol PM. We ate the cupcakes on the curb and I cried.

"It's too hot out," I said, my nose running.

The electricity had been shut off at Villy's. He said I was starting to depress him, so we both took three PMs as we walked the dark, lonely streets, as many stars in the sky as we had cigarettes left. Villy didn't care where we went, but I did. I led the sleepiest way as if we were crossing a time zone. Some movie where the plane flies over the ocean. The cabin is dark. Passengers' heads are slumped on strangers' shoulders, and it's impossible to tell if that is peace or the moment before the crash. At the swing set, the Atlantic rumbled a meshy white. Villy stood behind me with his fingers over mine on the chains. A plastic bag was caught in a tree branch, rippling and translucent. I kicked like I wanted to leave the world, because at the time I thought I could.

The other day I got a call from a telemarketer while I was unscrewing a lightbulb. I stayed on the line for forty-five minutes.

"As you may or may not know, Walker Oil is one of the best-known oil companies in Massachusetts, with a reputation for high-quality oil, excellent maintenance service, and timely delivery. Mrs. Adams, could you tell me if you use oil, gas, or electric heat at your home?"

I stepped down from the ladder. "We use oil," I said.

Outside the kitchen window, fresh snow, the swing set's slide a white tongue.

"Fantastic! While oil burners are fuel-efficient workhorses, they do need regular maintenance. Tell me, Ray, have you had your burner inspected in the past six months?"

"No," I said. "I haven't."

My daughter was watching something she shouldn't have been and laughed sadistically in the other room. I swung open the fridge to sober myself. Inside, a half-eaten PB&J sandwich.

"I would like one of our service people to stop by so that you can take advantage of our free inspection."

"To take advantage?" I said, my mind as white as the snow on the slide.

"Precisely," he said.

Earlier, chewing on that crust, my daughter had answered, "Good, not great," when I asked her how it tasted. It could not have occurred to her that an answer like that would hurt me.

"You could've just lied," I said, kneeling to look into her eyes, my grip making an impression around her wrists. "Say it was great."

# RAFFA

# BENNY'S BED

THE BUS DROPS ME on the sidewalk, which is full of veined leaves and crumpled receipts and soy sauce wrappers that scatter as if hurt when I kick them. It's the last day of school and I'm on my way home to lie to Rima's face for the five hundredth time. She is curled into the couch, *Caramel* flickering a lover's spat on mute. I tear off paper for a list, break the sharp tip of the pencil's lead, then look up to see Rima asleep. Her shallow breath is one with the fan. I put the list on her cheek, sweat blotting into pinpricks, but the wind takes it when the fan turns its head.

I click off the TV and pull the shades so it's dim. I wonder if everything was quiet when Benny was found slumped against the wall in a Laundromat bathroom. If I had been there, would I have run out the glass door into traffic, or would I have held Benny, wrapped my whole self around him in the bathroom, while the pink soap drizzled on the rim of the sink? Benny nodding out against the tile, his eyes rimmed old-wallpaper yellow. I think the laundry was spinning and chugging in each unbreakable machine when they found him, swishing wet colors that hurled against the glass when he died.

I wake up, sweat-soaked and stinking. We live in a one-bedroom, and Rima and I sleep butt-to-butt on a queen-sized mattress, our arms hanging off the edge. When I was little, she held me. I had nightmares that her arm was the arm of another. The arm of another coming to take me. I'd wake up gasping. I don't know when Rima stopped holding me at night.

I sit on the toilet seat with my hair clipped, cool water dripping behind my ears. I find Rima's cigarettes on top of the mirror, heavy with the lighter in the pack, then pull up the window to lean my elbows against the insect-littered sill. After I flush the butt, I hear Rima downstairs, plunking dishes into the sink. I pull on a tank top, the elastic frayed at the armpit.

"*Yallah*," she says, setting a glistening pan of baklava down to cool on the counter. I bite my nail, craving another cigarette. "Raffa!" she says, wiping the same spot on the counter in circles as if she'll get a wish.

"What?" I say, leaning against the doorway. She throws up her arms.

"What's this what?" she says. The corner of her lip twists where the mole beneath her nostril gives her dark eyes a crazed sparkle. She turns back and laughs into the counter, shaking her head. The sunlight from the window hits a strand of copper that sweeps through her still-healthy hair but she keeps it tied back in a scrunchie.

"So stupid," she says to herself.

"What's stupid?" I say.

She wrings a rag over the sink, quick and hard, the way she used to swipe brushes through the spirals of my hair. She squeezes till it's limp in her grip.

"You," she says. "You're what's stupid. Come help me."

"I'm going," I mumble. She turns back with a tiny smile as I hook my thumbs onto the straps of my backpack. She lifts herself on tiptoes to level with my eyes. The bright scars of her pupils readjust like cameras snapping for evidence. I think of her sitting puzzled at the dining room table, the way she used to stare at the Arabic-to-English dictionary, breaking pencils.

"Where you going? Huh?" she says, stepping back down. What could she know—nothing or everything? I blink. "Huh?" Rima says.

"I told you! Serena's." And like that, I'm out the door.

This is what freedom is. Each crumbling block between my apartment and Benny's house. The blue dumpsters behind our old elementary school. The woods in the arboretum, light spotting the ground, dazzling my arm. And up the giant rock, the size of a mansion, you can climb into the light where broken glass glitters off the top like a beach.

Benny hung out between the trees, down by the rock in eighth grade, the year we became friends. I used to hike up the rock and trample down to get home, where I knew Rima would be waiting for me with her head out the bathroom window, batting smoke from the air. Down through the branches, I'd seen Benny with his hood up over his eyes. Mickey had his back turned, spray-painting an outline of Marilyn Monroe midwink, flattened on the side of the rock. Benny tilted his chin up towards me.

"Hey!" he shouted, his hands punched into his pockets. Twigs broke under his stride. "Hey, *you*," he yelled, his face flickering under leaves.

Now the woods are empty as I duck through the twisted opening of the chainlink fence I leave rattling.

Benny's house is tall and brick. From the thick window of a car, it looks traditional, but if you're standing outside like me, you can see the front door is boarded up with plywood. Flowers with bent necks, thirsty in the boxes. Benny used to walk me through the side door after we'd been passing a bottle of Svedka back and forth on the swing set in his backyard. He would hold his palms over my shoulders from behind, and I knew he was pushing me to his bedroom, but it felt gentle, like we were floating.

Now I'm walking alone through the overgrown path towards Benny's backyard, past the rotting fence and the aluminum swing set and the piled-up bricks. I keep my hand on the knob while a full minute passes. It's unlocked. The kitchen is covered in blue carpeting and outdated appliances with knobs like old airplanes. Through the hall, like a portrait, Benny's mom is sitting in the living room on the recliner. Her hair is black and matted against the shades. She's watching an old episode of *Friends*. Relief passes through me like a slow sip of beer.

The first time I came over, it was my fourteenth birthday and Benny led me by the wrist past his mother passed out on the recliner and up the stairs to the attic. He never said anything about her. One day we were naked under his sheets except for the pair of orange polka-dot underwear I kept on, feeling like a Creamsicle, half to stay cool and half to tease Benny, who once said girls were sexier with their underwear on. We were having a staring contest. I was watching the yellow in Benny's iris blur to green as a tear slipped down my cheek.

I blinked twice and blurted, "Is there something wrong with your mom? I mean, why doesn't she say hello?"

"Who, Woman?" he said with a grin. "She's on lots of meds 'cause she's a *fuckin'* nutcase. Don't worry about her, though. Or me."

Benny pinched my chin as I pulled apart a split end. He didn't squirm. He was the only guy I knew with a beard, but the gap between his teeth turned him back into a kid. He floated his palm on the small of my back. A line, straight as the pills he snorted, charged up my belly button.

"Hi, Woman," I say, leaning against the dusty wooden stairway.

"Oh!" she says, reaching for her glasses. "I want to see you better."

Rima taught me to talk to strangers. Every time a new neighbor moves into the U of apartments, which is practically once a month, she pushes me across the walk to knock on their door. To shake their hand. She watches from behind our screen door, like I'm doing it for her.

"Raffa," Benny's mom slurs, slow as the hand she drags to her heart. "I'm happy you're here."

"I'll be up in Benny's room," I say, playing along.

The upstairs bathroom is airless. I run the sink, flipping open the mirror to find the Sesame Street toothbrush Benny bought for me at CVS. Across the hall, Benny's dad is watching CNN in his room. I know because he is always there, the door cracked enough to see the smoke drift like weather over his head. The only time I've seen Benny's dad out of the chair was last spring, when Benny and I skipped class to race up the stairs, tripping over jeans and belts. A half hour later, Benny's dad cleared his throat in the attic doorway. I stopped midstep so Benny tugged me too hard, and I stumbled.

"Shit," I said. Benny gripped my knuckles tighter, squeezing in some small part of my embarrassment.

"Hey, Pops," Benny said. He was beaming.

Before I can dash up the stairs, Benny's dad's face appears in the crack. I'm an animal stuck in the road. His pale eyes study me, a flash of Benny.

"How are you doing, Raffa?" he whispers.

I can't think, so I say, "My mom kicked me out."

"Ah," he says, rubbing the back of his head. My eyes shift. The branches above him are still outside his window.

Up in the attic, purple carpet, badly burnt from fallen ashes. A Bruce Lee poster hangs on the wall, next to a road map of the human heart. Benny's bed sits in the corner where the ceiling slants. There's a skylight over it, so if you lie down at night, you can watch your own episode of *Planet Earth* in this soundless rotation. I skim my finger over the smooth wood of Benny's dresser. I blow and watch the dust lose itself in the air.

I sit in front of the floor-length windows. Nobody can see me, but I can see everything. On one side, the radio towers out in Dedham; on the other, a faded view of the Boston skyline. I sit for a long time, waiting for something beautiful to happen, but it just gets darker.

I wait till it's totally dark to flick on the light, then pull open the bottom drawer of Benny's dresser. Under crumpled T-shirts are Benny's bottles of pills. I make a straight line of them on the carpet. Two of them hold tiny blue pills that rattle like Tic Tacs. The other is oversized with the label peeled off. White OxyContin dust chalks up the inside.

I stole the whole bottle once. We were having Serena and Mickey over, playing kings on the carpet.

"Two is for you!" I said, making my hand a gun aimed at Benny as he took a swig from his forty. Benny flipped a seven. We swung up our arms. Halfway through, Benny and Mickey crushed pills on Benny's desk with his school ID, then blew three fat lines as I pretended to braid Serena's tangled hair.

Benny found the bottle in my backpack the next morning, hidden in a sock so they wouldn't make a sound.

"Why are you so nosy?" Benny said as he pulled on a beater.

"Why are you so secretive?" I said.

"Stop going through my stuff, Raffa. I mean it. Those aren't yours." Benny ran his hands through his gelled hair. I propped myself up.

"They're not yours, either. They're Woman's."

"Relax," Benny said.

But I couldn't. Late at night I'd twitch from sleep to the sound of Benny creaking down the stairs. Woman kept her pills on the coffee table in a clear bin like a jewelry box. Separated into seven slots. Some of the pills were tiny and green as earrings, others pink ovals, the rest round and white as Alka-Seltzer. I'd sit by the stairs and listen so hard I thought I could hear the yawn of the box opening.

Back on Benny's bed, I tore my arm free from his grip.

"Stop hiding things," I said. "I know you."

"What's there to worry about, then?" Benny said. He wrapped his arms around me even though he was the one shivering.

"You're shaking," I said.

"You're pretty," he said. "So pretty it hurts."

I bit into his shoulder, salty with sweat. Benny stared at the floor and grinned, but it happened too slowly. Everything about Benny had become slow. His eyelids as they fell while driving. Even his skin looked slow, grainy and static as an old TV. The smell from his neck like a rotten vegetable drawer. He'd itch his arms like a kid. Eat discounted candy corn from the big bag.

All spring I calculated the missing pills. Forty-five down to twenty-six. Twenty-six down to eleven. Eleven to none. I'd know there was none when he'd pace around the room, then tear back to punch the wall without apologizing to me after. He'd stay home in bed, puking off the side or, worse, missing.

I get under Benny's covers and study the worn black letters of Woman's real name before the label got torn. I think about Benny's gap teeth and how when people die in movies, the camera swings up across the sky and sweeps through blowing leaves so they are everywhere. I don't feel Benny anywhere.

I wake clutching Benny's pillow. I refold all his T-shirts, roll the sleeves army-style like Benny would. I hang his button-ups, smooth out towels from his laundry. I line up his Vans, stick my hand in a dress shoe and find a torn wrapper. Suboxone, Rx only. In his desk drawer, chewed pencils and a spiral notebook. It's colored in on the first page with outlines of pinup girls and ghouls. I flip to the center where Benny writes over everything twice in bold lettering. I search for my name but get stuck on Benny's handwriting, all caps, severe.

*WOMAN IS OUT OF SCRIPTS!!!* It's December. He drove to Downtown Crossing in Pops's Jeep and found a homeless guy selling red roses on the shoulder. Three needles for thirty bucks if the bum taught him how to shoot up, with the promise of Benny taking him to the ER for the bad rash on his leg. Benny said shooting up wasn't as hard as he'd thought. He found a vein—this, the part that hurt most—ten orgasms at once.

Pots clatter downstairs. The sunny smell of burnt bacon hangs in the air. My stomach's empty, open, a cave. I slide my hands through the sleeves of Benny's button-up, drift downstairs. Woman is by the stove and swings back when she sees me standing in the doorway.

"You scared me!" she says with a spatula in her hand. Her black hair is clipped at the top of her head and piled high like a squawking bird could fly out. She wears fuchsia lipstick and a silky nightgown that skims her ankles. Benny's dad is at the kitchen table with the paper.

"You scared yourself," he says. I sit across from him and drum my fingers against the vinyl seat. Woman almost dances to the table with the pan, prying neon eggs onto my plate.

"Thank you," I say, holding a fork.

"Benny loves bacon," she says, heading to Benny's dad's plate. He sets the paper down, and for a second we stare at each other.

"That's enough," he says, and Woman thinks he means the eggs.

"Cha-cha-cha," she says, dropping the pan into the sink.

Benny's dad takes a deep breath as she shimmies between us.

"We had a dog once," Woman says. "Did you know that, Raffa? But"—Woman smiles but her eyes go blurry—"we had to give the dog away. I loved that dog." Woman looks at Benny's dad, her smile warped.

Benny's dad holds a napkin over his mouth and says, "Eat up."

That night, I wait until I can't see the radio towers in the dark. I go downstairs, same way Benny used to creak through the night. Woman's slippers are kicked up on the recliner and glowing in the dark. Her soft snore makes a sucking sound. I can make out the legs of the coffee table, the giant box of Woman's pills left open. Oxys are like mints, round and white. I'm holding four in my fist as I retrace my steps back up the stairs.

The next morning, I wake up with the pills still in my palm and dry-swallow all four. When I go downstairs to pee I stay on the toilet, my toenails half green since the last time I painted them. I stand in Benny's dad's doorway, where I see he is breaking kosher and watching the History Channel.

I'm high as hell. Fat bees hum lazily under my skin. Pops looks at me. I'm honey-warm and brave. Gray smoke twirls from his slack fingers, between the wilderness of stacked books and upholstered chairs. A big window seat facing the backyard surprises me. I hold on to the doorway. I'm wearing Benny's Bob Marley T-shirt and no bra.

"What's happening, Raffa?" Benny's dad says. I open my mouth to say something, but my throat sounds out a gasp.

"You want to watch this with me?" I nod. I sit next to him on the edge of the bed by his armchair. I skate my fingers through my hair and leave some pieces in my face. We're both quiet, volume low on a documentary about the Civil War. He holds his hands out wide on either arm of the chair with his legs crossed.

Benny's dad is going bald. I can see the outline of where all his hair used to be when the screen flashes gunpowder explosives all over us. It goes dark again, but when the gun cracks, I see the wrinkles that edge his eyes. His eyelashes long and soft like Benny's were. Like they're meant for collecting dust. I reach for Benny's dad's hand.

"Can you kiss me?" I ask. I'm frantic. I think I'm crying. Benny's dad doesn't flinch. He turns to me, both hands cupping my cheeks. I search him, his lips, half hidden by a longer beard than Benny's. He takes me toward his chest and kisses my forehead. Now I know I'm crying. We stay right like this.

Then I pull away from him.

I wander over to the window and hug my knees. The swing set looks small from way up here. I feel him watching me from his armchair.

I keep my head against the glass and say, "Did you know?"

Benny's dad keeps his cool. "No," he said. "People hide things."

"I knew," I say, fingering the cord on the blinds. Then I say something I've said before. "What's wrong with Woman?"

For the first time all week, I miss Rima. Six blocks away and alone.

Rima, I'm going back up to Benny's room for the last time. See Benny and me? It's freshman year. I'm on the bed with my cheek in my palm and he's standing above me wearing a beanie. You'd kill me, but I kneel up against his hips and twist it backwards. Neither of us blinks. Benny glides on top of me and cups both palms under my neck, then smooths back the hair from my eyes. He unzips my jeans.

"Will I bleed?" I whisper, and Benny whispers back, "You might."

He says, "Don't worry," his fingers tracing circles on my hips.

"Ow," I say, searching Benny's eyes. I hold on to my neck where my heart beats and grit my teeth. He shifts my hips over the sheets and tries from a different angle. My thighs goose-bump in the cold but are feverish with heat. I push his chest back slowly, impossibly, his knuckles making indents on the bed as he crouches over me.

"It hurts," I say, sweat leaking down my back. Benny takes deep, desperate breaths.

"Do you want to stop?" he asks. I shake my head, Rima, because I didn't want to be like you. Asleep when the sun's out, afraid to cross the walk.

Benny walks naked to his dresser, then yanks open the drawer. He comes back to bed with a closed fist, two OxyContins in his palm when he opens it.

"What's that?" I ask.

"So it won't hurt."

# WHEN I CALL,
# YOU ANSWER

OUTSIDE THE RAMADA, I'M engaging in a perfect parallel-parking job, mouthing *Whoa daddy* as I reverse into the spot. I'm cautious with my bumper. It's dented as the cans of beans Rima buys on the discount rack at Shaw's. The dent is from the last accident this year, my fault, so now this course. You know something is wrong when you are pushing thirty and have been forced to take a course on a Saturday. I rear-ended a Mexican woman's Kia after she stopped short at a yellow light.

"*Lo siento,*" she said from the curb, then cried into her hands.

The cop spat onto the grass and said, "Do you speak English at all?" knowing full well I was the one he'd need to speak to. I looked back at the crying woman and thought, *I'm going to lose my license.*

I despise cops, as well as teachers who think they are cops. In the last row of the driving course, I sit high-school style, twirling a number two. The *tsk-tsk* of the clock. The driving instructor looks exactly as you'd think. Like he's only ever read a book on the toilet. I ponder walking up to him, saying how I know he's been divorced, too. Why don't we both go home and sleep, hope we don't wake up? Exactly eight hours later I'm on my way to Rima's, disregarding every yellow light in JP. The best part about her apartment complex is the straight spaces. No parallel parking.

Nothing has changed about the kitchen, T.J.Maxx foldout table against the wall, the brick facade of the neighboring apartments crowding the window above the sink. The damp smell of oily dishrags and uncapped spices. Rima's in her little tracksuit with the rhinestones on the butt. She stirs goulash, then shakes so much paprika that it makes a cloud around us and singes my nostrils. I'm sitting like I never would have when I was younger, because I thought we were two women who looked alike and that's where it ended. Her, asleep on the couch, and me, running out. Rima turns back, gesticulating with the spoon.

"You gain weight," she says.

"Thanks, Rima," I say, pinching the flab that sits loose above my jeans.

"You gain weight, you lose weight," she says. "You gain weight, you lose."

"Sounds like balance," I say. Rima shakes her head, ladles stew into a bowl.

"You need to go out," she says. "I know someone."

"I'm good," I say. Ever since me and Mick got divorced, I've been coming home to eat from bowls, to take a break from what it is that has me feeling like a lost girl at the mall. Sometimes I stay the night and we sleep in her bed like when it was ours. I sleep dreamless, numb as Novocain through gums. When I wake up, I feel wrong and backwards, the same lost girl at the mall.

"You're good?" she says, scoffing. "You sit in that apartment with Serena eating cold pizza." She points the stained spoon at my head. "You need a job."

"I don't disagree," I say, spooning all the beef together for one giant bite.

"I have something," she says. "You go to the interview."

I'm pushing thirty and now is the right time to obey Rima. What I'm thinking is, *Do I have to buy office pants at the Gap?* There are primal-colored blouses on the racks, albino-white mannequins frozen midstride. I hide in the neutral section, tug a size two out from the bottom, and topple the stack.

"Can I help you?" a woman in a headset says. "I think you're looking at the wrong size."

She folds the pants methodically, keeps her eyes glued to my waist. I wonder if degradation was part of her training.

"I don't need help," I say. "I'm excellent."

Newbury Street on a Monday morning in March. Men in gray suits sporting backpacks, coffee splashing down their fists. I'm a honeybee, circling and zipping through the crowded streets for a space. I swerve like I missed an exit on the highway, an inch from running a biker off the road. The woman wears no helmet and has a blond child strapped to her back. Does she think this is Europe? Picking up speed in reverse, I nail a spot, tap a BMW's bumper, then reapply my lipstick in the rearview.

Inside the building, hushed voices echo off the swirled marble. The security guard motions for me to take off my bracelets and to drop my purse into the bin.

"*Merhaba*," he says, his dark eyes flashing from my bun to my heels as I gather back my things.

The building looks like a bank filled with my relatives. The security guy who checked me out resembles my cousin in Chekka, and the secretary before Selim's office looks like my aunt, dark-lipped and plump with a sugary smell coming off her neck.

Unlike my aunt, she's friendly. She swivels and grasps my hand. "*Habiibi*. I'm Lara."

"I'm Raffa," I say.

"You're here to meet Selim, yes?"

Selim's office is nothing like a bank. The carpeting is bright and there's an actual tea tray on his desk with turned-in picture frames and little metal horses that follow each other as if unaware they are headed off the edge. There's a smaller desk in the corner, empty and bare. Selim is standing next to it, and for a second I think he looks like David Blaine, short and dark-skinned with that magician's aura. He opens his mouth to say something, a gaunt and hungry look in his eyes, like he's calculating my ability to notice how he'll disappear.

"Sit down," he says, gesturing to the desk. I sit.

"Actually, get up," he says.

We do the reverse commute past security. Selim's got a swift stride, his sleek suit jacket slung over his shoulder. But I'm taller than him in my heels and follow closely behind on the crowded street.

"Sit down," he says again. I shimmy like an idiot. We're in Sonsie in front of the garage-sized window that looks out over Newbury Street, and the waitress is setting down menus in front of us.

"Give me an Amstel," Selim says. I let my eyes drop down over the menu. "She will, too. You're thirsty, no?"

I imagine the time is 9:30 a.m. Rima would be appalled. No one in my family drinks.

"Where are you from, Raffa?" Selim says.

"Jamaica Plain."

"Where are you from, I mean, in Lebanon?" He sits back in his chair, smirking, his inky eyes reflective, unsearchable.

"Oh," I say. "I grew up in Jamaica Plain, but my family is from outside Beirut."

"I see," he says. "And what makes you want to work for me?"

The guy has a point. The Amstels are set down on crisp napkins. Selim takes a sip and his silver watch flashes.

"I speak Lebanese," I say, feeling clueless. "I can write in Arabic, too."

"Let me tell you something," Selim interrupts, holding his bright palms out, the only place on his skin free of hair. "My last secretary didn't know the fax machine from my asshole." Jesus. He sips. "If you learn quick, we can work together. I've heard nice things about you."

I bring the newly critical Amstel to my lips and take a thirsty gulp.

"You will research the economy in Beirut, keep up to date on information coming from Lebanon. You manage my contacts and talk to people who have difficulties obtaining visas, passports, and so on. We work with different resources in Boston. Now, let me ask you, what do you think will be your most important job?"

"The research?" I say, impressed by my ability to retain information.

Selim laughs deeply. "You're hilarious," he says. "When pretty girls are hilarious, it's a winning combination."

"What's the most important job?" I ask.

"You're available to me at all times. When I call, you answer. If you're in the shower, you call me right back."

He slugs the rest of his beer. "And you'll learn to make me a good tea. Okay, get up."

That night on our sunken couch, I bite my nails as Serena files hers thoughtfully, then holds the file up by her delicate cheekbones.

"You drank beers at breakfast?" she says.

"That's not even the weird part," I say. "He watched me make him tea, just to test my instincts or some shit."

"Is it a Lebanese thing? You know, treating women like maids."

"Maybe," I say. "Did you know my dad wanted a boy, and when I came out, he wouldn't hold me?"

My phone rings and I seal myself in the kitchen to pace.

"Nice job answering," Selim says. "We're doing good so far."

Forty-five minutes of lecture (next week he'll test my Arabic, I'll organize the computer system that tracks his schedule by the minute, he'll teach me the intricacies of consular notification so that when I meet with citizens I will be able to explain the process).

Serena peeks her head in. *Pizza,* she mouths.

I shake my head, send her the worried-eye lock we give when we're in trouble.

By the second week of working for Selim, I've learned how to beat traffic by not joining it. I'm switching lanes down Storrow and catching some long Bostonian honks and a couple middle fingers that I have no trouble mirroring.

"How is it?" Rima says over speakerphone.

"I'm late," I say as I cut through back roads towards Newbury.

"Well, don't be," Rima says.

"Rima," I say. "How do you know Selim anyway?"

"Don't worry about it," she says as I cheat a stop sign, inciting the *zoop* of a cop car. The officer, fingers hooked in his Santa-like belt, approaches my window, then bends down as I crack it.

"Any idea how fast you were going?" he says disaffectedly.

"Just write the ticket," I say, nodding towards his pen.

Selim slams the phone down as soon as I shuffle in. He's moved my desk directly in front of his and he's got his hands on his hips. *No bueno.*

"Why are you late?" he says.

"I was driving down Newbury Street. I was, like, almost here. . . ."

"Okay, forget it. Just sit down," he says.

I sit at the desk. There's a notepad in front of me. Selim walks over and presses his fingertips into the stained wood.

"I need you to jot out some things," he says, "for the meetings we have before noon."

Here is why I can't eat the other half of the pizza Serena orders at night with extra-extra ranch and a sickly-looking sliver of cheesecake. I said I could write in Arabic. Didn't say I could write well.

Selim points to the pad. "Write: Oath, any form of an attestation by which a person signifies that he or she is bound in conscience to perform an act faithfully or truthfully."

I pick up the pen and make, of all things, a star.

"So, write this in English?" I ask. I am certain I will wind up crying in front of Selim, but now cannot be the moment, so I concentrate on the star.

Selim adjusts his tie. "What do you think?" he says. "What do you honestly think, Raffa?"

"I'm guessing . . . Arabic?" I say.

"You guess Arabic," he says. He begins to clap. His final clap sounds like he's dropped a Bible and I flinch. He presses his fingers into his eyebrows. "Don't tell me you can't write in Arabic."

"It's been a while. I need a little bit of practice? I don't know certain words."

"So, do you always lie like this? Are you always full of disrespect?"

"I wouldn't say that," I say, then think of a summer in Chekka at my aunt's house. Dirt roads and concrete houses, the Mediterranean Sea the color of spat mouthwash. Fruit the way it should be, strawberries the size of grapes and tomatoes sweet as cherries. My aunt sacrificed a goat on Sundays. It hung as the dark blood pooled in the divots of the hot grass, swaying with its arms tied as the carcass gleamed a fatty white. She'd eat the cooked meat under the tented table as I snuck off. The night breeze sent me up to the roof, where the scoop of the broken pool sank like a skating rink. I'd lie by the drain and call Benny on my aunt's flip phone, halfway around the world. He'd tell me that he loved me more than anything as the phone broke up his words.

I didn't hear about the phone calls until the month after I came home, when Rima called her sister, who instructed her to put me on the line. I sat on the stoop, listening to her broken English for over an hour, my cheeks still hot from the raw Chekka sun.

"You have such disrespect. Where is your heart? Did you lose it? Tell your mother, how does it feel to pay all this money long distance?" she said before she hung up.

"Here's what we're going to do," Selim says. "Stay here while I have my meetings. Call my wife, tell her I will be staying very late tonight. Meanwhile, you're studying."

He goes behind his desk, rummaging through drawers till he finds what he's looking for. He slaps a yellowed English-to-Arabic dictionary on my desk, thicker than the textbook at the driving course. He writes down his wife's number, then stalks out with his jacket trailing over his shoulder.

On the other side of Selim's desk is a black-and-white photo of her, Selim's wife. Another relative-looking woman with dark untamed hair and eyes a thousand secrets deep. She holds a baby girl, her eyes tightly shut against her shoulder. I hold the photo in my hands while the phone rings. I explain to her who I am.

"Raffa," she says, "don't work too hard for Selim. He can be a little much, but he means good."

A month into the job and I've made a habit of calling Rima every day before and after work. It is the most we've talked maybe ever. One day she doesn't answer, the next day, and the next. On the fourth day, after I leave the office weary from staying late, pretending to accomplish the impossible, she picks up.

"Come home," she says, and tells me she's making lentil soup.

"You're skinny," she says at the front door, tugging at my blouse.

"Where have you been?" I say. "I've called you ten times."

She smiles like a scarf thief. "I went to Lebanon," she says, her face hidden above a pot of bubbling lentils.

"Are you kidding?" I say.

"Why do you ask me that, are you kidding? I met a man. We talk on the internet. We like each other. I go to see him."

"Rima," I say, "since when do you date?"

"Think about this. I meet him at the airport," she says. She sets a steaming bowl down in front of me. I push it away.

"Are you starving?" she says.

"I have nerves," I say.

"Why?" Rima says.

"Just finish the story," I say. There is no way to explain how working for Selim makes me feel like there is a finger jabbing impatiently at my chest as if it is a button on a stuck elevator.

"I meet him at the airport. Raffa, he stinks! I'm telling you." She takes over the room with her hands and bats away his breath as if it still lingers in her face.

"Stinks! I fly fourteen hours and he can't fix his hygiene? That's it. I'm on the next flight home." She grips her hands on the side of the table.

"You're out of your mind," I say.

"I'm crazy, but you have nerves because you're thirty, you have no husband, no babies, and you're too skinny now."

"You're rounding up," I say. "And I don't want another husband."

"Why are you always so stupid?" she says, smacking my wrist. She picks up a handful of cashews, then throws them into her mouth and starts cackling. I look at her sideways and take a deep breath. She's got a point.

Selim feels at the height of his powers when he is ordering at restaurants. A month and a half as his assistant and we've had lunch at every place on Newbury Street. Selim has religious tendencies when it comes to lunch. I make the reservation regardless of how busy the place gets. We leave the office at half past noon and I walk a step behind Selim on the sidewalk in total silence. Selim motions to my chair, pulls it out with curious politeness, tells me to sit, and then proceeds to spend the entirety of the hour asking me questions that make the hair on my arms prick as we sip on two Amstels each.

"Selim," I say, "they're not criminals or animals or anything like that. They're refugees. They have nowhere to go."

"I didn't say they were, Raffa," Selim says, opening his palms. "What I call them is intruders. Potential terrorists. Worse than animals. Push them to the border, get them out of Lebanon."

"You have no soul, Selim."

"What do you know about having a soul? I have pride in my country. You don't care about where you come from. Your mother helps you with a job and you don't even appreciate it. Lebanon is still home, you know."

"What do you know about my mom?"

"If you care to know, we went to school together in Beirut." He looks at me with that persistent stare. "But you don't." He shrugs bitterly.

"She doesn't tell me anything," I say.

"A box for this," Selim says to a passing waiter, pointing to my untouched sandwich. "What are you trying to be, a model?"

You gain weight, you lose. I'm down ten pounds, or whatever number it is that has my office pants in need of a belt.

The next Monday, I sit at my desk without Selim telling me to be seated. He walks in front of the desk and starts laughing like a maniac, clutching his stomach and stamping his foot as if putting out a fire.

When he gets ahold of himself, he asks, "What did you do to your hair?"

"I dyed it," I say. Serena did. We were distracting ourselves in the aisles at CVS and came across a hair swab that Serena tugged from the rack, then held up to my roots.

"You look like an idiot," Selim says. "Like someone poured a bucket of bleach over your head."

"Yeah," I say. "That's essentially what happened."

If it wasn't for Rima and my trips to Chekka, I'd think Selim was insulting me, but I'm cursed with the knowledge that Selim is only pointing out the truth. I'm reminded of a conversation I had last week in Rima's kitchen.

"Oh, Americans think the truth is evil. 'Oh my god,' they say. 'That hurts my feelings. Oh my god!'"

"Rima, that's why I never had my friends over. You told them they wore too much makeup. Or that they had boyfriends because they had low self-esteem."

"They do!"

Another curse that comes from working for Selim is that my writing has improved. I'm able to write in Arabic more fluently. Short sentences, even if I sound like an eight-year-old. It has me daydreaming sometimes when Selim is sitting behind me typing, and I'm jotting things down from the dictionary, things so basic and rhetorical but translate awkwardly. *Call me. Go away. Answer me. Come back.*

Something goes down midweek. I misread a fax from an important client, and for the rest of the week, Selim's cranky with me.

"Answer the *fucking* phone!" he says after a single ring.

I get up and walk out of his office as the ringing proceeds, swinging open the door past Lara's desk, who looks up at me as she sets down a jelly doughnut. She follows me to the bathroom, and when we're safe inside, she hugs me, her breasts a soft pillow.

"All men are like this," she says, looking at me fiercely. "They're *manyaks*."

I know what it means because it's Rima's favorite word, too. I don't know whether to be relieved or not, because I don't actually believe Lara. Not all men are dicks. I wish it were that simple.

The rest of the morning I avoid Selim. I'm sick of his phone calls at night, literally, Serena feeding me Pedialyte from a spoon. When she holds up a Dorito and crunches, I can feel Selim's voice on my back. How I jump when he slaps a stack of papers onto my desk from over my shoulder.

Quarter past noon hits and I'm back to typing and Selim is on a long-distance call with a diplomat. I quietly gather my coat from the rack and break past security into the April beat of a busy morning. I stop into CVS to ponder a mascara, hyperaware of how ordinary I feel. I want to collect the feeling in a bottle just so I can spray some on later. Serena meets me at Panera and we wait in line for ten minutes, kids with juice-stained upper lips a few feet below us hanging onto the firm hands of their mothers. We sit by the window with our trays. I bite into a turkey club, bacon and everything.

"So good," I say.

"Yes," Serena says. "Eat mine, too."

"I can't do this job anymore," I say.

"No shit," Serena says. "You need more Pedialyte than a day care."

Serena knows something about quitting. She quit her teaching job and then her babysitting job, and now her job is keeping me fed. A man slides into the booth next to me. Selim. Serena sips her Pepsi with a stunned look. He reaches out over the table to shake her hand and holds it about ten seconds too long. Goddamn dramatic.

"Nice to meet you. I'm Selim," he says solemnly. "Raffa's boss. I'm sure you know me."

Serena stays silent, keeping her eyes focused on me with the worried-eye lock. I turn to Selim.

"What are you doing?" I say in a low voice.

"That's my question for you," he says.

"You followed me," I say, the lunchtime chatter swarming through my head.

"You ran off," Selim says. "I'm in charge of you. Don't think you can just run away and I won't find you."

I shift the tray and smile nervously. "I'm not a child," I say. "Okay?"

"Just remember what I said. You can't just get lost. I'll come find you. Anyways, nice to meet you, Raffa's friend."

Marathon Monday sets Storrow into a frenzy of arrowed neon signs and police officers on steroids barricading the roads. I'm going eighty in a forty-five on the detour and thinking of how my fear of Selim is turning into my fear of a new job, of starting over again. Rima calls and I pick up.

"Why are you working today?" she says.

"Good question," I say.

Newbury Street is blocked completely, the marathon finish line tented in the distance. I park by the Common and walk the ghostly backstreets, the office like the bank on a Sunday, the security guy forgetting to check me out, then nodding at me sleepily. Lara at her desk painting her nails a murderous red.

"What do you need done today?" I sigh, ignoring the ritual pouring of Selim's steaming morning tea.

"The question is what do I not need done," Selim says without looking up. "You should know by now where to start."

By eleven we hear the sounds of a crowd gathering below the window, cheering and whistling lifting louder like a rising fog around the office. A sudden applause roars through the windows.

"I think a Nigerian just won," Selim says from behind me, and I roll my eyes freely.

"Well, we can't leave for lunch," I say, savoring the oversight.

By the afternoon, there's little to do and we're starving. I'm full of outright contempt, like a grounded girl. Nobody is working today. Selim is just keeping me here because he can. He yawns and I want to reach behind and backhand him.

And then the noise, a sound like the street cracking apart, three times over. I turn back. Selim has his hand on his hip by the window. Another crack and Selim's arms cover his head. The window blows apart. The glass a blur of thrown-up light as it screams past Selim, who is running towards me.

Selim, who wraps his arms around my shoulders and tackles me to the ground, and then we crawl out the door to hide under Lara's desk, where I look up to her crying, the phone coiled on the floor. Beside it, laying on its side, is one of the metal horses from the edge of Selim's desk. We wait for who knows how long. The sound of sirens cuts like lasers through the office. Selim keeps his hand on my shoulder as I rock myself back and forth. Noises from the street sound as unpredictably as a jazz record. Selim swipes blood from his forehead, which looks like a can of paint with the drips dried down the side. He keeps his palm on my shoulder protectively, even though the office is still now. Lara picks up the receiver. Her daughter tells her that we should evacuate.

"I'm leaving," I tell Selim. "We can't stay under this desk."

"You're not going anywhere," he says. "It's not safe. We have to stay here."

Selim's breath is milky from tea he made himself and his eyes are intent under the dimness of the desk. I am literally on my hands and knees when I say it: "I quit."

"Don't follow me," I say. "Don't!"

I duck up from under the desk, pulling down my skirt as I wobble away. Selim shadows me down the empty hall. I take off my heels and start to jog till we get to the abandoned security desk, the marble cold on my feet.

"Selim, I don't work for you anymore." I back up towards the door, my heels held tentatively in my fists.

"It doesn't matter," Selim says.

"What did you say?" A hot day in Chekka when I was too little to speak, the sun in my eyes. I remember Rima crying into her hands under the tent. Crying because my father would not come to see us. Because my father had disappeared, and Rima lived her whole life inside me.

"I said listen to me." Selim's eyes go vacant.

"Is that supposed to mean something?" I back up to the door and Selim nods.

I want to fly fourteen hours over the Atlantic through fat clouds and watch the low blue swirl as the plane nears. I want to walk through the Beirut airport with my head held high as I drift towards Selim like in a dream. Only to pivot roboti-cally like some fucking model. Out of spite, just like Rima. I want to fly home with my mouth hung open, sleeping dreamlessly. If Selim is my father, I don't want to know. I do not have that dream.

I turn back coolly to the double doors of the building with my palms up and crash them open. The sidewalk is white with the sun's savage sparkle. I walk in slow, vulnerable steps past ambulances parked crooked, strewn plastic cups, the garble of radios on hips until a cop grabs my elbow. I want to rip my arm free, say fuck off, walk alone, but in the street a man lies in neon running shorts, his body surrounded by EMTs. They kneel in their dark pants, scissoring his shorts clean off.

I let the cop take me, and as we pass I see the running man's head cocked to the side and still, darkened by blood. I walk with the cop quickly, letting him guide me away. He leads, all the way down the stairs at Park Street into the dim station, where all we hear is the scrape of the rails and a rumbling forward. He holds my elbow firmly until an advancing train bullets towards us.

The doors open, then close in the time he releases me, before I can turn to see his face. I make my palm a cast around my forearm, holding on to it so carefully as if it is broken. The window whips by shades of blackness, blurred concrete, the eventual flicker of light and greenery. I walk all the way to JP, to Rima's, the only place I can think to go.

On these quiet streets, in the weird warmth, I see my spectral self. The nights I ran out for sumac and onions, blue ink from Rima's list on my fingers. Then older, with a backpack, running away towards the woods. Birds cross through branches, ghost into the depths of leaves but tweet like jazz, unpredictable, alive. At Rima's, I fumble with my spare till she rips open the door, squinting and pissed. I look into her eyes, see a whole world between us. And myself, her whole world.

She yanks me in by the wrist, but I am ravaged by the absence of his grip.

# SERENA

# HOW I DANCE

**IN THE HOTEL ROOM,** I hold the champagne like a rifle and aim towards the glass painting. A pastel sunset so boring I could shatter it. Before I can say "I'm kidding," James grabs the bottle, shakes it, then pops. We show up to the reception a little buzzed off the champagne and Coronas from the hotel's ice bucket. Dad is marrying a woman named Leona. It's polite to call her a woman—she's only two years older than James. She works as a waitress at Dad's new restaurant. The room is filled mostly with her relatives, a DJ with half his head buzzed into the retarded shapes of lightning bolts, and a photographer who waves us together at the table for photos. I want to explain, say, "Excuse me, sir, but I don't know these people." Even their laughter has an accent.

The rest of them are Dad's people. Rio back from Miami, who recalls my height the last time he saw me by gesturing to the floor. Sharkey, who sulks at a table in the back and does not look at me with his bloated face. I pivot towards the bar and order three gin and tonics. "Strong," I say. I make sure no one's watching and down one, two. I bring the other to James. We wander over to the vinyl dance floor. It's the prom I never went to, a hundred silver balloons bumped up against the ceiling.

We trail our hands overhead to catch strings. I pull a balloon down to my chin so it taps my mouth, making the balloon a microphone. Lip-synching "Let's Stay Together." James spots me across the crowd of strangers who dance like a bunch of Sims on coke, then reaches up to tug down his own string. He's Bono, holding the string down with his foot like a mic stand, all open arms and balloon flapping like wind while he lip-synchs with conviction. I pull down a new string, wrapping the thin ribbon around my neck, silver balloon head floating up. I hold both hands over my throat, tongue out, my eyes crossed in a choke.

James dies laughing.

From here I can see Leona cutting steak, my dad's arm outstretched across the delicate crisscross of her chair. James whips down a string, pulls it through his legs, then giddyups, trotting across the dance floor to the bar. He signals the bartender for two more stiff drinks. I yank down a string and hold the balloon to my belly, smirking at James. He holds a hand over his eyes as he sips out of the tiny black straw. I'm in labor, hiking the silvery balloon up my dress, the semen-colored head popping out. I wail, make like I'm about to faint. A little crowd gathers around me, shuffling to the beat. They snap their fingers to a Three 6 Mafia song and assume I'm the one with problems.

James kneels down to where I've fainted and takes the newborn from my arms. He cradles it. We bust up laughing, an inaudible cackle against the speakers. He extends his arm above us, fake camera in his hand as we pose. I'm propped on my elbows, the lighting making spots against tablecloths. My dad kisses Leona on the hand as they get up from their table.

James pulls down a string so he is face-to-face with his wobbling opponent, like "What, what," then head-butts the balloon. I gear up both arms like a Bowflex, pulling two balloons down against my chest to show off my new boob job. James mouths, Ew! as I release the strings from my fingers, the dance floor turning a soft LED red.

A slow song comes on and everyone turns as Leona lifts her dress, then wraps her arms around my dad as he dips her back slowly. Turned upside down, she is truly beautiful, with milky skin and a Colgate smile. It's polite to call her beautiful, when there are other things I could say.

I draw down my last string. James is pink-faced, tie swung over his back, staggering with his gin and tonic, waiting to see what I'll do next. If my dad looked at me, just once, instead of brushing his nose against Leona's, he would see me nine years old. If I were a photo, he could have written on the back of it: *Serena, Balloon.*

But I bring it to the floor, grind my heel against the string to keep it down. I give the balloon mouth-to-mouth, cheeks thinning, a paler silver. I want to show how I can save a life. I blow till there are tears in my eyes. It's so beautiful to give something all you have, to try. But now most of the couples are clutching each other as they slow-dance, taking turns raising eyebrows at me over rotating shoulders.

I look up at James, scream, "Help!" My voice distorted and squeaky with helium. James dives down to the floor, pumping his palms in CPR as the rubber shrivels in my cupped hands. The music cuts as the DJ tilts his head. The dance floor is silent until a sound like chipmunk laughter rushes up my throat. I slump onto James, searching the eyes of the crowd. Eyes all around me, conscious as cameras. Eyes that don't believe my emergency.

# TELL US THINGS

MOM WAKES US UP in the middle of the night.

She says, "Hello, my sleepyheads," and, "Baby, I know." She says, "Hold still," as she tugs coats on over our pj's, then takes us out to the driveway and buckles us into the van. She says, "Brrr!" from the front seat. We wait, chattering our teeth, till the ice melts on the windshield.

On the drive into the city, Caleb slumps asleep in his car seat. I sit next to him and poke at his veiny eyelids, open them slow so his eyes flutter up. I imagine he's dreaming about bottles, coffee tables, all the things you get to see, crawling around on the carpet. When he starts to fuss, Mom catches eyes from the rearview. My hands go back in my lap.

It's so boring, to drive and drive in the dark past the Citgo sign. James and I stay awake the whole ride. We say, "Tell us things. Tell us stories."

"Be specific," Mom says. She looks back at us with her eyebrows up.

"I don't know," James says.

I say, "Love story."

Mom tells us the story about how she met Dad when he cooked at Icarus, but we already know how it goes. Parts I remember most are how Dad wore suspenders when nobody else did.

"Crazy guy," Mom says.

"How crazy?" we ask.

"Hmm, messy-hair crazy," she decides. She turns the wheel, Fenway all green lights and empty sidewalks. Dad walked up to her table on New Year's Eve.

"Dark and tall," she says. "Like you'll be, Jamesy."

James rests his chin in his palm, his pinkie dug into his lip. Dad took her walking late at night and showed her Sam Adams statues in the Common. There are only a few cars on the road. Mom turns up the heat.

We wait for Dad in the back parking lot. Mom rests her knees against the wheel, the snow piling up on the dash. When you're opening a new restaurant, you have to work very hard, and everything is very. Very hot, very late at night, very sorry we are so very sleepy. Waiting for my dad to come out takes forever.

"When are we going to be home?" I ask.

"Do I love you?" Mom says. She waits.

I nod, yes, and she says, "Then you are."

Mom tells us the story about the day I was born. It snowed four feet that cold night in March. Dad was cooking at L'Espalier. Mom drove herself down the same snowy roads we drove through to get here, past the Citgo sign, Fenway, and the dark water. On the other end of the phone, Dad said, "Call her Snowy." Like how he wanted to call James Mookie if the Red Sox won the series two years before. But he was too late. She'd named me Serena. Nothing to do with the storm.

She turns back to give Caleb a paci, but she's run out of stories. The guys standing by the back door are crouching on milk crates, flicking cigarettes. Dad comes out the back.

He says, "Attaboys!"

They say, "See you Jef-AY."

They stand so he can pat them real hard on the back like he's saving them from a choke. Then he climbs into the front seat of the van. The light comes on. His shirt is stained with red splotches. The door slams as he leans back onto the headrest. It's dark again as the car fills with his scent: soy sauce, onion, sweat. Mom looks at him gripping his hair back as she's pulling out. If he shook it, flour would dust his shoulders.

On the ride back, I copy James. He's really asleep. I fake dreams to seem more believable, letting my head hang on my shoulders with hair in my face like Cousin Itt. Streetlights on Mom's cheek when we pass over the bridge.

"Please," Mom whispers. "If you did it then, you'll do it again."

"Goddammit," he says. "Shut up. Just shut up."

Mom turns off the bridge and I know we're taking him to Columbus Ave. She parks and the lights come back on. She turns, holding up a finger because she knows I'm awake. They walk up the steps to the door of Dad's new apartment, but I can't see them past the gate. The orange *click click click* of the van wakes up Caleb when Mom rushes back with a scarf around her mouth.

Mom takes us to the new restaurant for dinner on Friday night. We take the T eleven stops. She wants a picture of James and me outside Rocco's, but it's freezing.

Mom says, "Act like you like each other," as she waves us closer together.

There are too many people walking past on the sidewalk, and I don't smile, not once. We walk up dark wood stairs and sit in a black booth in the back. It's our booth. Dad told us so. It's raised so you can see the whole scene through pillars: a bright blue rug with confetti polka dots, tables with handcrafted roosters and pigs, men in suits who sip on dark drinks and women dangling forks over their plates, and the highest ceiling, higher than our church's. Dad and Lester Levine hired painters, and they stood on ladders for weeks drawing old naked angels that Dad called rococo and Mom called Gothic, then insane.

By Christmas, famous people are coming into Rocco's. There's frenzy by the door with Marco, the doorman who looks like a CIA agent. Roxanne stands at the front in a black skirt. She leads people all around. She weaves through tables with a big black menu held tight to her chest. Everything about her is black. Her hair, her huge dark eyes, her bra strap. She smiles when she sees us and twists down in her skirt, shaking a tin can of lollipops. Mom waves her off and pulls us forward, saying we're not supposed to talk to Roxanne. She's here to work, not to talk to us.

But I like Roxanne. I want to talk to her. In the fall, she took us to the Science Museum on a Tuesday while Mom cut hair. We took the T and passed Northeastern, the school she goes to. We put our hands against the glass to see dinosaur bones and then curled up in our seats for the movie. The lions on the giant screen licked their cubs, carried them with their teeth by the scruff of their necks. Later, in the bathroom, Roxanne slipped a lipstick out of her purse and bent down, her necklace hiding beneath the buttons of her shirt.

"Make your mouth an O," she said, her eyes crossing over my lips as she sketched. "So pretty," she said, then hoisted me to the mirror. I pressed my lips, they parted pink, and I saw it. I was.

At our booth, Mom scoots us all the way in. Sometimes we eat with rock stars or Red Sox pitchers. When Harrison Ford came to eat at our table, we lay on Mom's lap while a white screen dropped from the ceiling. We watched a black-and-white film of a prom from the fifties. The girl dancers swung back smiling and looked like Mom without the color, the way she laughs with her tongue between her teeth and holds people close, your heart like a sponge in her hand.

"Those are called poodle skirts," she told me, her breath tickling my ear.

I whispered back, "Who is Harrison Ford?" Everyone laughed.

Tonight, there are no famous people and I'm glad. Mom runs her fingers through my hair, fans it out across my shoulders. "Can I cut your hair, baby?" she says.

She's wanted to cut it all year. She wants to give me bangs. Short, like Gidget, but I won't let her. I want my hair to grow back long so she can braid it like she did when I was little.

"Nope," I say, shaking my head as my hair flies free from her fingers.

Sharkey comes to our table and holds out a tin can full of crayons. James and I pick out our favorite colors, and he gets all the good ones: forest green, jet black, navy blue. Sharkey waves waiters over to our booth. They bring us cheesy flautas that we lift to our mouths as the goo dribbles off the plate. Sharkey works for Dad. Dad's the boss of Sharkey, but Sharkey's the boss of everyone else. Sharkey isn't his real name, but no one here has a name like Sam or Bob.

"Ugly picture, Rena Bird," Sharkey says. He kisses the top of my head, then leaves his hand by my neck. I get shivers in my middle, the way I did when Roxanne dragged the color across my lips. And secretly, I think Sharkey is a funny guy, because he's handsome, in the way only funny guys can be. He's pale like me with blue veins through his forehead. I'm trying to draw his face on the back of my menu with a white crayon, but I can't make his blue eyes look like the ocean when the water creeps toward your feet. And I can't make his hands move, the way he talks with them, like Italian men do, but he isn't Italian—he's straight from Ireland like Mom. We watch his hands as he leans over the side of our table and sends us colored plates.

"Eat, eat, eat!" he says, with his apron folded over at the waist. He tries to make Mom laugh when he says her name. I look up at her when she does. Her laugh doesn't sound like other ladies'. She gets breathless and hits the table with her palm, her eye wrinkles wincing. She gets pink. Caleb bounces his knees on her lap, his tiny fists gripped tight around her fingers, spit dripping from his only tooth onto her jeans.

If Sharkey were my dad, I think he would be sitting next to my mom in the booth, instead of leaning over the side of our table. James and I would face them, and Sharkey would hang his arm over my mom's shoulders like they were in high school. He'd watch her get pink. He'd let Caleb wrap his fingers over his and he'd lift him into the air like Caleb was a superhero. Sharkey would butter my bread and call me Rena Bird, and I wouldn't be mad about it anymore.

Inside the restaurant the candles glow in the whites of eyes, but downstairs the kitchen is like a different channel on TV. It's easy to crawl out from under the table, freeze like you're going to be caught, then sit quietly on the stairs with the rubber mats and bits of lettuce. I'm expecting for someone to pull me up by the arm, but the cooks are all scrambling around in aprons, bumping into each other. They wear backwards hats, wiping sweat from their foreheads with their shoulders. Stoves and refrigerators match knives and pans. Steam blows from a pot as knives smack through meat onto wooden boards.

Dad holds a giant pan's handle with a damp cloth, red sores spotting up the length of his arm. Tape on his knuckles and a stub where his thumb was sliced clean. The pasta in the pan flies up as he flicks his wrist and catches it back, fire underneath like a ghost's jaw thinning down electric blue. Dad's head is bent but his hands are quick and moving, pinching salt from high above a plate. He chops an onion to bits, stirs and tastes sauce with a wooden spoon.

Lester the owner skips down over me on the stairs with his heels clicking. He puts his hand on Dad's shoulder, but Dad keeps working. Lester has white hair like a priest. Dad says Lester treats him like his only son. Lester fostered him when Dad was James's age exactly. He sent Mom and Dad to St. Martin for a honeymoon, and bought the house we live in on Kenney Street. Dad stirs and chops, Lester behind him looking red-faced.

"Have a glass of black champagne," he says, holding up his wineglass.

"Church is in session," Dad says, waving Lester away. He turns back to the counter where a pig in black sunglasses sits dead. She's belly-down on the cutting board till Dad flips her and thrusts both arms into her stomach. He hacks her ribs out one by one, cleaning the bones till they're dry, going from the belly to the shoulder, cutting her into smaller and smaller pieces. Then he gets to her tail, the rag over his shoulder spotted with finger-streaks of blood. Rio brings me a strawberry, and I chew through to the stem.

Dad yells over his back, "She's going to be a tasty baby, ain't she, Rio?" Rio smiles his sweaty grin. His checkered pants are held up by plastic wrap.

"Yes, cheffy!" Rio says.

Dad yells, pointing to plates. "Sexy those up."

Rio and the others circle him in orbits, bringing him plates and olive oil. He points to the stove and Rio leaps to the pot. And like that I'm found. Dad sees me on the stairs. His eyes searing through smoke. It's quick, like if he had a camera, he could shake a Polaroid, watch me appear. Take his Sharpie to the back, *Serena, Stairs*. But he turns to the burners.

When I close my eyes, I see Dad and a circle of fire he can't get out of. Flames from the explosion. I see Lester Levine held from his ankles on the top floor of the Four Seasons, a muscled guy yelling, "Where's our money?" His clicky shoes falling to the concrete twelve floors down. Just like Dad told it.

At Dad's last restaurant, a strange man ran down the back stairs during prep. Dad called after him, but the man darted into the alley. After the last plates went out, he was wiping the counter when a big boom thundered through the pipes. Everything burned. A policeman held back Mom from the tape. Jewish lightning, Dad called it. Everything in ashes.

"Did Lester need money?" I asked, chewing my straw at Bruegger's the next week. James glanced at me, then back up at Dad.

"He didn't need it," Dad said. "But he was after it."

No one found me. It's dessert time and Mom's sipping coffee. James and I hide underneath the table, Mom's bare ankle bouncing. We are shadows through white linen. We bang Matchbox cars, flip them off the ramp of the leg. We slip Mom's shoes back on.

"Look," Sharkey says. He finds us under the table, crawling under with a striped rag over his shoulder. He's cupping one hand over the other.

"Hurry," he says. His pointer finger is covered with drippy chocolate from the downstairs stirring bowl, big as me, and he says, "Taste it, Serena," like a dare. James watches me in a squint. I'm the only one who gets sweets.

Tuesday comes. Mom cuts hair at Studio 27 and Dad has to watch us. He picks us up after school on the court by the redbrick wall where James's friends fight till there's blood in the snow. I stay close to James, late like all the Metco kids who wait for buses.

"I'm Ambrosia," says an older girl. "What's your name?" When she smiles, her braces sparkle.

I lie and say, "I'm Snowy."

We walk home in the cold. Dad walks ahead, taller than the basketball hoop in our backyard. He keeps a hand hidden in his pocket. James walks in front, Dad in front of James. Caleb's nose is red from over Dad's shoulder, the sky dim and orange. Before we get to go inside, Dad opens the back gate and we shrug off our coats. Our backyard is small with the rusty basketball hoop and the chain-link fences.

"Go back and do it again," Dad says, his voice even. He keeps our time as we sprint, pacing with his watch up by his throat. "Again. Impress me."

We kick up the slush, crash our fingers into the fence, then turn and run back. I'm slow in the cold. It burns my throat. The fence feels farther every time. My arm buzzes when Dad yanks it. He bends down so I have to look him in the eye.

"Who's the prime mover?" he says. "Huh?" When I don't answer, he shakes my arm. "You, you are. You understand what I'm saying?"

Dad picks up a frosted football, runs backwards, then spirals it towards me. It drops between my arms. I toss it back lazily. Dad sends it back spinning.

"Let it come to you!" he says as the ball bounces hard against the frost. "Let it come to you."

In the garage, Dad lifts weights and listens to sports radio from the boom box, and there are only two boxes left, frames wrapped in newspaper. His leather jacket, dirty baseballs, weights and spoons and Bob Dylan cassette tapes. When I was smaller, Dad held out his arm on the bench in the garage and flexed, his T-shirt torn at the armpit. The hair there curled like the tail on the pig, only his was dark and wet.

"Feel these muscles, *chica*," he said, and I traced the hard lumps of his arms. "These are to protect you."

Then he'd lift me onto his stomach on the red bench. He'd hold my hands over his hands on the shiny pole, then hike the weights off the handle, lower the bar all the way down to my chest till it touched. We'd push the bar into the air together, all the way to a hundred as "Hurricane" played, his armpits stinking like onions and the tip of my hair wet from that sweat. Last week I took that tape from the boom box he unplugged. Maybe he'll think it got lost. Or forget he had it in the first place.

Mom comes home and we run to the door. James holds her scarf. We fight to hang it. She sits on the stairs, unbuckling her heels. She smells like hair spray when I'm in her arms. She pecks every part of my head.

We sit at the table and Dad stands over it. Floorboards creak like a hungry belly. I can tell because he's quiet. And when Jamesy spills his milk, Dad yanks him from the chair and rips off his shirt. Makes him eat without it.

From the table, we hear the garage door slam and then the clink of the weights spinning on the handles. The harder the weights slam, the more Mom smiles. Her teeth a darker and darker purple from wine. Mom whispers, like a test we can ace, "Everybody name one good thing about their day."

James looks up at her. Caleb says his first word: "Mum-ma."

It's late when we drive Dad back to his apartment on Columbus Ave. I sit in the back seat and stare out the window. People in coats cross the walk when it says Don't Walk. Mom ticks on the blinker. Outside the fast window, black branches reach like fingers, then pull farther apart. We pass the train tracks by Northeastern where pretty girls sit on benches wearing earmuffs and striped scarves. On Dad's street, Mom slows down. A guy walks into Dad's building with a case of beer over his shoulder. Dad leans over to kiss Mom on the cheek, but she turns to the window.

"We'll see you next Tuesday," she says, but it sounds out a question.

Instead of going home, we drive all the way to Lester Levine's in Newton, where all the one-story houses have big lawns and long driveways and front doors with potted plants and bronze doorknobs. Mom tells us to wait, to be good, no dumb smile, then comes back with an envelope she tears apart with her nail.

We walk with Mom down the cereal aisle. She tells us we're going to take a picture with Dad for a magazine called *Food & Wine*. Caleb waves his arms out from the cart, blabbering to Mom, who says, "Hi!" I throw Lucky Charms into the cart, but Mom takes it out. I throw another box in.

"Who cares?" I say.

James smirks at me from across the cart, his backpack half slung over his shoulder. Mom looks at me the way she does when I'm poking Caleb's eyes.

"You didn't get that attitude from me," she says. "Serena?" I toss another box into the cart. She bends to touch my arm.

I get right in her face, grinning so she smiles back, like when I'm going to kiss her. I narrow my eyes.

"Shut up," I say, still smiling.

She pulls her face back, her mouth hung open where all her dark cavities are. She puts her hand on her cheek. James takes her other hand.

"Don't cry, Mom," James says. I walk ahead, trailing my hand over the rows and rows of bright boxes.

"Shut up, shut up, everyone just shut up," I sing as I smack one off the shelf.

Mom leans over the sink and scrubs. She wipes, dusts, sprays, and sweeps. She takes us to Filene's Basement. In the dressing room, she drops to her knees to button James's new shirt, her purse hanging heavy on her wrist. She twirls me in a zipper dress that itches and pricks. The mirrors triple her smile. It makes me want to cry, but I don't.

"You can cut my hair," I say. She bends to cup my cheeks. She wraps my hair all around her finger till there's no more of it and asks me if I'm sure. At home, I sit with my arms hanging over the kitchen chair as the water from her spray bottle trickles down my neck. Dirty-blond hair falls to the tile by her painted toes. When she's done, she takes me to the bathroom and holds up a hand mirror. I keep my head down, then peek. I have bangs.

"I'm sorry," I whisper, then bury my head in her shoulder.

Dad and photographers come to our house. They take over the kitchen to set up lighting and big black equipment. They take test shots of Dad cooking omelets. He moves around like a robber, sneaking a butter knife out of the drawer and slipping a rag off the handle to keep on his shoulder. He waves me over from where I'm waiting by the doorway.

I go to the stove. He rests his hand on my back. He hands me a piece of cheddar cheese, then lifts me up by the waist in my velvet dress. I drop the cheese. The ends curl up yellow in the heat. We flip the omelet in the air together. His hands over my hands on the handle. Burning hot but it feels nice on my palms.

When it's time to take the picture, we all stand behind the counter. There are green plates in front of us with mint leaves and diced fruit. The photographer angles us together as Dad wipes oil from the edges with the rag. Mom holds Caleb up to her cheek while James stands by her hip. They fit. The photographer switches lighting and move us around.

"Come up," Dad says, the way he orders sous chefs around in kitchens. Outside the window it's snowing hard, the trees sagging and white.

I say, "No."

"*Chica*," he says. "Come up here now." He tries to pull me, but I twist out of his arms and sink to the floor.

"Serena," Mom says. I start to shake and cry.

"Leave her alone," Dad says. "She's a baby." He cracks his knuckles. "You want to act like a baby? I'll treat you like a baby," he says. He yanks me up and I go flying into his arms. He squeezes my waist, hard, like he's trying to hurt me.

I wrap my arms slowly around his neck, my eyes burning as I watch the snow erase our backyard.

The photographer changes a bulb and turns my chin to the lens. It takes forever. We have to look right.

Dad stares straight into the camera. His chin is up as the photographer holds fingers in the air. All the while I'm thinking how I want to be called Snowy. How I'll be eight in two days. All I want is to be forgiven.

"Beautiful, right there," the photographer says, and snaps.

# CALIFORNIA

NIKO WIPED SWEAT WITH his collar, then left me with the tattoo guy, who slid a stool under his legs. My nose was broken for the third time. Everything I saw—and I saw everything—contained the swelling's shadow.

"Sure you don't want to know?" the tattoo guy said.

"No," I breathed. "I don't."

Tattoo guy contemplated the veins splaying down my forearm, blue as the alcohol in the jars.

"Never done this."

"Even better," I said. The choice was his. It was arbitrary, yeah, but you can't say I didn't decide. Later, at the patio for happy hour, Niko would point to the beer I'd like. The waitress would scan our menus, her eyes flitting to the wrap of plastic on my arm.

"Do you read?" I asked him.

"I like Melville," he said. He was tracing, then rubbing the practice words clean with a rag. Thinking of something worthier.

He lifted my arm like it would drop, then rolled back on his chair to inspect the evenness of the words. He swiveled to wipe the needle. I assumed he was satisfied. We caught eyes, our necks flinching. Then he found his way back to my arm, stretched my skin taut. The tattoo guy looked a lot like Niko before he started wearing button-downs to cover the tie-dye look of his sleeves, though he was his own boss, sold high-end electric guitars to kind of famous punk bands. I taught first graders how to write their loopy names on lined paper and had the entire summer off.

"A kid died in Southie," I said. "His mother left him in the car."

The tattoo guy tucked his hair behind his studded ear, teeth bit over his lower lip in concentration. A drowning woman twitched on his arm, black waves, squids siphoning up her ankle. He wore his sleeves like medals.

He said, "Having children is child abuse."

Niko had gone off, disappearing into the heat on a mission for cigarettes and cash. He'd kissed my throat, in front of the tattoo guy. Without him, I felt the relief of the AC, the sweat that ridged my wife-beater drying out on the nerves of my neck. The heat wave outside had me pressing ice to my eyes. Dogs suffering on chains type heat. The kind that would make our beer boil on the patio.

"What if I'm writing something obscene?"

"I don't give a fuck," I said. He winced like smiling could kill him. A long time it had taken him to apply that design. A long time it had taken me not to look. I wanted not to know: what I thought, what was there. Now it was happening. He was engrossed, shading me black, his thumb pressed to my pulse. The moan of the needle revved, he steadied his hand, and the pain, like his hand, was delicate. It was a finger in warm wax, hardening. A careful carving. Nothing like getting hit. Blow by blow in bright, ecstatic cracks that fainted like fireworks.

His ink was a slow, low dose, milking through my blood like a capsule. I liked the bounce of the needle, smooth as the wheels on a plane when it skims the tarmac. My arm his paper and the drone through his fingers a blossoming. We were cheek to cheek. I didn't fidget. When I did, it was towards him, as if he were pulling something out of me. He turned back, one gloved hand still hooked to my arm, and soaked a cotton swab in alcohol.

He could have been drawing the outline of California: the state you think of when you think of escape. The date: July Fourth. Line from a book: *Call me Ishmael.* Bobcat: the knowing eyes. Old lyrics: "I'd like to help you in your struggle to be free." With his hand like that on my wrist, I thought of clothes packed in a bag to the brim. The clothes in my mind were always neat and never mine.

# NATALYA

# ENGLISH HIGH

**IN DAYLIGHT, IN DORCHESTER,** she's not ghetto, no matter how hard she does or doesn't try. Here, the shootings make newspaper headlines in the *Globe*, the paper she used to read aloud to Mona, despiser of English. Here, drive-bys and homicides don't rhyme like the lyrics on her mix. Behind the wheel, Nat's face is round as a dinner plate. Pale and bloodless. Caterpillar-green eyes made greener by black liner.

Dorchester is the ghetto, or that's what Serena calls it. Nat drives past the MSPCA sign and the bus stops and the Dominican barbers who sit in front of the windows in folding chairs no matter the weather. She makes the tires wail at a red light. Raffa cranks the volume and they sit transfixed, mouthing, *Murder She Wrote*. A flake of snow hits the windshield like a bug and dies. The barbers claim the corner, sway their jean-slung hips. Metal picks stick out the sides of their heads, their hands outstretched in the white air. Nat feels the bass on the wheel as the barbers limp toward the rumble of the Intrepid.

Nat looks elsewhere as they circle the car, dropping their coats, the flash of an armpit. Hands cupped to the window, their breath making marks. Her eyes straight ahead, the color of frozen grass, their Soviet coldness. She revs it and the barbers jump back at the hips. Through the red light the street blurs, one green eye in the rearview. Serena leans forward from the back seat, the corduroy fabric like a couch from the seventies. Her arms splayed like she's flying.

Nat parks outside the Laundromat on Dot Ave. Boarded-up storefronts, aluminum doused in graffiti. Police tape whipping in the wind. A woman with a gummy crack-mouth hobbling past, singing. Outside Lucky Supermarket, an abandoned swivel chair wrapped in plastic, the coil hanging cut on a pay phone. A kid in a Sox cap and an oversized tee stands on pegs to zoom through the intersection, yanking back his handlebars to pop a wheelie.

Raffa lights a cigarette.

"Put that out," Nat says, watching the kid pedal back. The cigarette arcs out the window and she imagines her fake ID jumping the same way, out of her back pocket like a fish in open water.

On the street, they're a music video. A flock of slow motion. Glass from busted-up windows crunches under Nat's worn Nikes. Serena redoes her ponytail, a neon elastic in her teeth. By her feet, a guy sits slumped by the peeling green bike rack, a black beanie pulled over his eyes. He holds a piece of cardboard, *Omar, Army Vet*, in his stoic hands.

The door chimes. Nat doesn't recognize herself. The delayed blur of three bodies on the surveillance. The tightness to their T-shirts make their hips look like bottles of cheap perfume. They swing open freezer handles, keep their backs to the clerk, who stretches over the counter like a cat, blowing wax off a scratch ticket. Nat fingers the cash in her hand, soft as Mona's pajamas when she was small enough to climb into her bed.

Nat leaves the liquor store with a thirty over her shoulder, snow dropping hard then, like dollar bills from a game show ceiling. Feeling victorious, she slips the extra bill in the homeless guy's empty DD cup.

He lifts his beanie, his name in her throat two thuds: Victor.

Back in the car, she slides the thirty under Serena's calves, her fingers numb from the shock of the cold. The cold of the shock. Raffa clicks a lighter as a cop taps a knuckle on the window.

He lines them up on the freezing curb, collects their IDs, his boots crunching in front of the Laundromat. Victor is now standing, leaning against the bike rack, watching the cop scrutinize the fakes.

"Where are you from?" he says, then cranks his neck to spit into the gutter by Nat's shoe. His accent is movie-thick, which only means he's from somewhere outside Boston, like Chelsea or Revere. Nat keeps her elbows propped on her knees.

"You going to answer me?" Nat looks up at him, his cartoon jaw. She wonders if this is what having a father is like: "Are you going to answer me? Do you think I'm made of money? Don't talk back to your mother."

Just in time, "What's your father's first and last name?"

Nat lets out a choked laugh. "I don't have one."

The wind swirls the salt on the sidewalk. By the brick of the liquor store, Victor is gone.

Blue salt in the Best Buy parking lot. The smell of heat and exhaust each oncoming dark, when the yellow and blue lights kick off. Nat failed school last fall. Four F's stamped down the page, a broken-looking C in English, one useless A in photography. The report card was waiting on the table between the salt and pepper shakers. Before Mona kicked her out. The only things she remembers from the fall were the pictures she printed: Mona chopping lettuce bitterly as kitty threaded between her ankles. Serena smiling secretively in the back seat. The bats and moon blue of the sky in Dedham when she drove down the highway, the feeling of fleeing. A barstool.

On Saturday, Nat wakes in the back seat of the Intrepid, her breath sour yogurt. There is crust in the corners of her mouth, half-moon shadows under her eyes. In the wet stalls at Best Buy, she pees for fifteen seconds straight, then uses a mini toothpaste to squeak her teeth with a finger.

She drives back to the Dot, across the highway where the skyline obstructs the fluff of clouds. She drives and the buildings get taller. Dorchester a maze of addicts crowding the shoulder lane with red roses in their hands, the look of static TVs flashing in their eyes like marbled, broken channels.

On Dot Ave, she sits freezing in nothing but jeans and a hoodie, afraid to waste gas. She nibbles at a waxy stick of licorice. Her nipples feel raw, pinched. Sore as her broken rib. For a second Nat *is* Boston, ancient and tense.

She looks at the bike rack, but there are no bikes, nobody.

By noon she's picking at a cyst on her forearm. The gunk beneath the bump strains against a thin piece of skin. She tears it with her nail, white pus shooting onto the steering wheel. The divot on her arm fills with oily black blood. Mona would have slapped at her wrist, told her to quit picking. And if Nat picked anyway, Mona would take her to the clinic on Centre Street to see some short Indian doctor, who would gauze her. The bill would sit on the kitchen table between the salt and pepper shakers for weeks, like "Look what you've cost me."

Nat presses her shredded sweatshirt sleeve against the wound, then looks to the sidewalk. She recognizes the beanie first. Victor walks out of the Laundromat with a magazine tucked under his arm. She thinks to turn on the ignition, follow him down the street. But Victor just stands outside, blocking the wind with a cupped hand to spark his light.

He looks much older than the last time they were together. When Nat was fifteen and he was twenty. White smoke escapes from his mouth, and when it clears she notices his cheek, gruff and pocked. His ugliness like a diamond, clear and cut. He walks, stops, sniffs the air.

Nat turns the key and Mona's scratched CD plays on full blast. "Barcelona"— she's been listening to Freddie Mercury for days. "*I had this perfect dream. . . . The dream was me and you.*"

Victor looks at the car. Nat kills the volume, then leans to crank the window. The cold makes her cough. When Victor leans his forearms on the door, she swings her eye to the rearview. Cold eye, monster green. She hears Victor tapping the hollow metal of the door.

"Got your own car, all grown up now," Victor says. "I saw you here last week."

"Yeah," Nat says, feeling a foot away from herself. "We got busted."

"Saw it." He smiles, his teeth opalescent as sea glass. The cold sun everywhere. Her tongue stuck like bread caked to the roof of her mouth.

"Let me in?" Victor says.

The car fills with his scent, something oily like vanilla. He leans back into the window. He's not afraid with his eyes, trying for the full view of her. His lips bright and open as a wound.

He fishes a pack from his pocket, then slips a cigarette into Nat's fingers. She smiles with her mouth closed, not knowing where to go but driving anyway. He holds the cigarette with his thumb and forefinger. He doesn't blink as the smoke spills from his nostrils, his eyes on her cheek.

The next day is different but the same. Route 9. They drive and smoke and stay in their heads. Nat imagines Raffa and Serena walking through English High's halls side by side, buying Doritos and red Gatorades from the vending machine in the caf. What if they were talking about her behind her back? And Nat would never know. She'd never want to.

Victor shields his arm in front of her at the gas station like he's saving her from a crash. It's odd because she's parked. She watches him at the pump. Sunlight warms the wheel. Nat wraps her hands extra tight as she pulls out.

"I should be hungry," Nat admits. Hunger has her stomach split like a knife wound that opens and hollows, then closes in on itself.

At the diner, the stiff-haired waitress pours them two thick milkshakes for the price of one. Victor forks home fries onto her toast. Nat goes crazy with the ketchup. The pileup of food in her stomach breaks apart her nerves.

"Did you graduate MIT?" she asks.

"Nah," Victor says, his palms out flat on the table. "Some things came up I had to take care of."

"I'm supposed to be in school today." Nat waits for something, for his palm to meet her cheek, but he just stares.

"You should go back, flunky," Victor says.

She sips and the cold shake numbs Nat's tongue, melts, then turns sweet.

The ignition goes choppy as they wait outside English High like fugitives. Dirt under her fingernails, nerves skipping like a scratched track. Nat unbraids her hair, then rebraids it. Snowflakes pick up outside. They're slow to fall and pretty. She kills them off the windshield. Raffa clicks the front door open, and Victor gives a wave. She shoots Nat a look, then slams the door, climbs into the back.

"Hey," she says, blinking at Nat in the mirror. Nat pops the DC, hands it to Raffa, who lights a 100. She smokes moodily as Serena climbs in the back.

"This is Omar," Nat lies. "He can buy."

"Hey," they both say as they gaze out the window.

The Intrepid hums hungrily as Nat drives slow down McBride Street.

They cackle at the sophomore girls who wear North Face jackets and Tiffany bracelets. Nat imagines their bank accounts brimming with bat mitzvah money, their after-school snacks on a white granite kitchen island. The staleness of the smoke mixes with the crisp air from the cracks in the window. In the rearview, before Nat tears off, she notices the way the light assaults the silver on their careless wrists.

Outside the packie where they first learned to Hey Mister, Nat hands Victor thirty quarters for three forties and a five-dollar bill for a six-pack for him. She watches him carry the bottles to the counter.

"Who the fuck is this busboy?" Raffa says, hugging the headrest. Serena snorts, catches Nat's eyes in the rearview, then sighs and chews a nail.

"Shut up," Nat says, letting a small smile grow.

Victor slams the door shut, then leans back to dispense cigarettes like gum. Nat turns up the mix: *"You a industry bitch, I'm a in-the-streets bitch."*

At a red light, Nat cracks a paper-bag PBR and hears the hiss in her heart. Her ex-boyfriend Erik drove a Range Rover and taught her to drive. He slouched back in the seat with one arm hanging over the wheel, the other over her. Nat drives back to JP in the same fashion, freezing PBRs in the cup holders, her one free arm around Victor's seat.

The thing about being ghetto is that toughness is a kind of love. By now, they've driven everywhere but home. She makes a turn onto Tremont, the snow brightening the road. She passes the Planned Parenthood that sits back off the street, its womanly purple walls. She passes her old apartment where she and Mona lived in government housing, before Northeastern bought their old brownstone for student dorms. Nat slows. She was fifteen in the old place.

Nesting doll on her windowsill, painted wooden cheeks getting smaller and smaller until the blush was just a dot. Blood slipping down her legs in the shower. And the fire escape where green leaves flitted soundlessly against the window like fish tails. Victor from next door went to MIT and smoked blunts on the railing, her bedroom window cracked in spring against the radiator's hiss. After Victor handed her the blunt, she coughed for five minutes straight. High, the traffic noises below sounded like video games, and the dirty-white flowers reeked of semen.

Victor twitched his nose, the silence loaded as he savored the rest of the blunt. Mona worked long hours at Macy's, so Nat climbed through the window behind him. His room was identical but opposite to hers. The door on the other side, the windows switched. She was the one who slid off the condom, wanting nothing between them. Not even a song on the boom box. Just the sound of the fan lashing the air. Her own grunts and sighs like some haunted girl begging in another language. Her jaw hung open to mirror Victor's, not from awe but from the promise of awe.

Once, in Victor's bathroom, she watched a drop of blood expand in toilet water, thinning, then blooming. Once, she wore his unwashed T-shirts and they went downstairs to Anna's, where Victor paid for two super steak burritos, then pulled up chairs in the very back. Nat listened to him talk about his biochemical engineering classes as she folded her tinfoil into smaller and smaller shapes. Every minute or two Victor glanced around. She knew he was nervous about being seen with a girl as young as her, her face so pale it blued, though she had promised she was sixteen.

Once, she moved her bed against the wall where Victor slept adjacent. More than once she held her hand up and left it there. It reminded her of her father in Ukraine, if you can be reminded of someone you'd never met. The way Mona told her the blacklist kept them separate.

Every street reminds her of something. Tremont will always be blood so bright it shocked her. Her hand on the wall where one night she heard a girl's voice murmur in sighs on the other side. Or the day they got caught, when they were messing around in Nat's kitchen, Victor pouring pineapple juice in his boxers. Nat took his free hand and slid it up her shirt. She braced her back against him as he fingered her spine. The keys popped the front door's lock. Mona stepped into the doorway of the kitchen before Victor could dart past her. She held his shoulders and yelled so violently in Russian that Nat imagined her screaming at some other man. Victor moved without a word, his name on the mailbox taped over. The absence felt seasonless, a hollow pain so widespread it kept her fingers numb through summer.

Nat drives the length of JP twice. Victor keeps his hand hooked to the garment handle. Train tracks divide the cracked road. Frozen T windows refract the blur of colored bar lights. Golden arches, a shopping cart hitched on the curb, the church's brick wall a spray-painted scene of a gospel choir midbelting. Seventies thrift shops with black ribbon necklaces. Thin, fragrant blouses screeching on the racks. Dead flowers under loose glass that Nat nailed to her bedroom wall where her hand had been.

These are their streets. Rainbow jimmies in a wax cup for eighty extra cents. The ice-cream truck's nauseous ballad. Mozart Park, swings, three in a row. Hot rubber on her ass where her shorts skimmed her butt cheeks. Winding, tight streets. Nat's street, where old ladies wear scowls, fur coats, and stark-white tights. Where Berezka's sells olives and zefir and there's a McDonald's next door.

Nat passes her apartment and thinks of Mona in the kitchen. Picky with the grocery list and making borscht on holidays. Nat's aunt furious with her stiff napkins. Her apartment is across the street. In Ukraine, she was a scientist at a university. Here, she's on Medicaid. Her hall of clutter is unbearable and the windows only let in soft gashes of winter light.

In Chernovsty, they lived with Nat's father. Eighty-six square meters and books in the bathtub. Mona worked at a toy store, then a watch store, then a veteran's deli. She only tells one story. May Day, before Nat was born. How she walked to the parade. The shock of stepping in puddles with neon streaks.

Nat winds through the rotary by Arbour Hospital where the road turns off wider. Lawns stretch from houses like long, taunting tongues. The reservoir has a weird shine, a trick of black fur on a bird's wing. The hills climb higher, arts and crafts Victorians stilted behind white fences. A Whole Foods on the corner. Cottage cheese for six bucks, the kind Mona likes with the pineapples. English High on the other side of the Arborway. She circles the loop around the school for the fun of it, her tires sloshing puddles and spinning out on residential streets. She jerks the wheel to make a turn in the road where there are no turns, the street warped with dirty snow. Victor is smiling, half his face slit like the moon.

Outside school, triple-decker houses at their back, they can see into the gym, whose lights stay on through the night. The rims of the basketball hoops ready, open jaws. She doesn't want to think about last year or next year, how college moved towards her, then broke apart like an iceberg.

She lets Victor pick a reggae station, then takes his arm and slips up his sleeve to study his forearm. It's smooth. She takes his other arm but doesn't find what she's looking for, track marks. How he's ended up doesn't make sense. She used to watch him sketching a double helix, strands that wound around each other like wind spinners. He once quoted Rumi, took her to a used bookstore in Cambridge.

"Why'd you drop out of college?" she says, wanting to unlock his mind. See if it's as cluttered as her aunt's apartment.

"I got someone pregnant," he says, then shrugs.

Nat's sleeve covers her fist. She takes a long gulp of beer, not feeling the freeze of the spill until it sops into the puffy layers of her jacket. She has feelings, but the carbonation pulps them together. The pit of her stomach fizzles like milk flooding a bowl of Rice Krispies.

There is distance between the rows of empty seats in the stadium of the gym and where she's sitting now, in the driver's seat. She stumbles out and finds her footing in the mounting snow around the tires, pissing in the glare of the headlights.

Victor wants to show her Waltham, where he grew up. Ice cracks off the windshield on the highway. He signals the exit, pointing a two-fingered gun to make a right, dirt sealed in his fingerprint. His thumb split like a gash made of wax. She swerves.

"Pull over," he says. "I want to drive."

"Can't," Nat says, risking a glance. "This is my dad's car."

"You don't have a dad," he says.

"You weren't in the army."

"You're drunk."

She sees them fighting in a room with no furniture. He touches her face beneath an underpass. Pushes her in an empty shopping cart, swings her around at the brink. She's thinking of next week, the food stamps they could split and the days with no hours.

Earlier, in the Shaw's on Tremont, she and Victor put together two fives and strode inside, shaking packets of M&M'S like maracas. Sampling a gummy California roll from the deli counter. Before they bailed, a girl with a crooked headband blocked the end of the aisle. When they came close, the girl looked up from just under Victor's waist. She twisted her legs.

"Hi," Nat said, crouching at eye level with the girl.

"I can't find my mom." It was only when the girl looked up at Victor that she began to pee, her pale pink leggings darkening in streaks towards her ankles. Victor held his hands in front of his chest as if he were pushing off a weight.

"We can't help," he said, taking Nat's wrist, steering her past the girl.

Nat pulls into the parking lot of Victor's old apartment complex. The lot is straight and lined like a bowling alley. Void as someplace like Phoenix, beige as Ohio. Different from the harsh lights of the Best Buy parking lot. Victor in the passenger side with the seat cranked back, his head to her feet on the couch of the back seat. She wakes in rushes of cold to the rails on the T rumbling like giant marbles sliding through a wooden room, then climbs into the driver's seat, where everywhere is bright, obstinate morning light, clean and cold. She waits for Victor to wake up, even though there's never anywhere to go. Nowhere in Boston. Nowhere in her mind.

She listens to "Barcelona" on the lowest volume. Decides that the best love is something that can ruin you like permanent eye damage, spots of darkness in everything you see. And if love is a person, she'd gun them down in the street. She pictures herself in the paper that maybe Mona would be forced to read.

In his parking lot, Victor palms the hair back from her forehead on the couch of the back seat, the streetlight orange film. He looks at her, glides his hips over her hips. She looks away, the way she did after she dropped him a dollar and he lifted his beanie.

It's impossible. To look someone in the eye in this way. She gets it from Mona. She has one photo of her father and Mona together. Soviet Russia, 1989. It must be perestroika because her father, the history teacher, is not working, the school burned to the ground. He's sitting unrelaxed at a dinner table in a Puma T-shirt. His face is scarred down the right side, a white line like a tear. His arm stretched over the back of Mona's seat, where she sits with her hand under her chin, her eyes looking through the wall as if she sees something beyond it.

If they look in love, they don't look at each other.

Victor turns back her chin, firm, like he's been teaching her how to look at him her entire life. She looks at him thumbing her bra, his teeth pinched around her nipple. She feels the pressure of his thumb on her jaw, the place under her ear that aches, that is locked. She puts her palm against his chest and presses. She lifts his hand to mirror hers.

"See," she says. "We're making a pact."

"Looks more like a prayer," Victor says.

"It was a wall," she says, feeling the slap she'd been anticipating. She draws her hand back. In front of his face, it glows futuristic orange. The power seems to come not from the light, but from the tips of her fingers, her identity. Nat stretches her hand out, and more power builds. She studies it, the seams stitched by light. Like if she kept holding it, pledge-like, it could be scanned by some machine that transports you. She thinks to wave it, goodbye, then wonders where she would go.

# STOP IT

**THE WORSE THE SNOW** fell, the faster Seamus drove. He was drinking Cuddy's from the glove compartment, darting between lanes, the tires drawing up slush when he swerved.

"You're making me late," Seamus said as he revved onto the exit. I kept my backpack between my knees and was hoping we would crash. We didn't, but a week later, my rib would be so broken that I wasn't able to breathe without tearing up. It had me wondering about luck, if we'd have been better off crashing. To have walked along the silver straight of the guardrails, chilly and scratched, until I saw something I recognized.

I was trying not to look at my green eyes in the passenger mirror. Or his cheek, the purple shiner from his blackout. Seamus worked ten hours a day, six days a week changing oil. He thrust open hoods covered in frost and barked orders to his ex-con employees, who called him boss. In his blue Dickies, his knees came up to the wheel, even with the seat cranked back. It was impossible for him to look injured.

I couldn't reach him the night before, and had shown up at his place with a peach in my hand. He lifted me to the counter and bit in, the juice running freely down his chin as Gerry hurled a bottle at the trash can beside us and missed.

Safe outside school, I draped my arm over Seamus's two-door and said, "Can we go to the movies?"

I wanted to see this one that was out about Micky Ward called *The Fighter*. I thought Seamus would like it. We'd never been on a date alone. We'd only gotten slices of pizza on double paper plates, or breakfast sandwiches with drip coffee on the mornings after, Gerry nodding out between us in the booth. Or at the dive betting Keno, Gerry strewn across the back seat in Seamus's car, the waffle of dirt from his boot on the window.

"Maybe New Year's Day," Seamus said, spitting dip into his foam cup.

"We'll be too hungover."

English High looked like a legal building. You only knew it was a high school because outside there was a smokers bench, where kids with blue hair and pale skin huddled together, their jeans torn at the crotch.

My counselor up on the second floor was waiting, stroking his tie. I was in BRIGHT for skipping class, so every time he saw me, which was mandatory, he played up the drama.

"Welcome," he said. "Have a seat."

He wore sneakers with khakis. He liked to mispronounce my name. He called me Natalie. He said, "Natalie, this could very well be your last chance."

The patterned tie he wore was an arrow to his crotch. He asked me if I knew my grades before this year combined with my SAT score were good enough to get into BU. I asked if he wanted to pay for it. He tipped his head back, cradling it with his palms, the wings of his elbows suggesting the expectation for a blowjob. I knew men like this, who wanted me to be afraid. I wasn't. It was senior year, right before I dropped out, and at the time I thought there were always more chances. I just sat there in his office, smiling.

Up by the lab, it was warm with the heat piping through the dusty vents. I passed the corkboard before my classroom where our teacher let us tack up our most interesting photos once a week. Most were cliché black-and-whites of the Boston skyline. In mine, concrete came in rocky like a close-up of Saturn. It was just a walkway littered with electronics. You had to squint to see the busted-up TV in the background, tilted and out of focus.

There was no one in the darkroom. I was alone with that vinegar smell pooling out of the basins. I clicked film out of my 35mm and wound it up in the total darkness of the canister. I waited for the reel to dry on a clip, holding the negatives up to see all those translucent moments like X-rays going one by one. Under the enlarger, I already knew which one I'd like.

Beneath the fixer, Seamus appeared, his scally cap, the chaos of yellow backscatter on the bottles behind him, the hooked impression of his dimples, his foot tipped on the barstool.

The next week was another chance to go to the movies alone. We woke up hungover on Seamus's pilled mattress. Facedown in his pillow, his hair was mashed against his head like a field of grass that'd been paraded on. I was in his Celtics jersey and nothing else.

He flipped over, said, "Ow," to the ceiling fan.

"Homemade water," I said, stepping on Seamus's car keys on my way to the bathroom. I sprayed the mirror till my reflection dripped. With toilet paper, I wiped in perfect circles, watching as my face reappeared. Seamus was tossing on a beater when I handed him water.

"Today is movie day," I said, on the mattress to be as tall. A stupid spin lifted my shirt. Free show. I jumped, my throat between the blades of the fan.

Seamus said, "Jump again," then threatened to flick on the switch.

I went limp, measuring his glance.

"Calm your liver," he said. He went to kiss me, his tongue flicking mine like a snake tasting the air.

"I'm making you eggs," I said.

Seamus went, "Don't forget coffee," then swiped the back of my legs to break my balance.

Out in the living room, Gerard was where we left him on the recliner, his feet kicked up and his mouth wide open like a scrawny security guard who dozed off during a robbery. A blanket with *Cape Cod* and the outline of a lighthouse crocheted across it covered him from the neck down. Gerry used to work at Best Buy till he got fired for drinking on the job. Then he got a job bartending at the Draft but was fired there, too. He got bagged on a DIP, lost his license, and had a Breathalyzer in his beat-up Buick. Seamus got him a job at Jiffy. When I asked him why, he tossed his cigarette in a snowbank and told me there's nothing he wouldn't do for Gerry, that hopeless fucking Mick. That skid.

I kept my eye on Gerry as I whacked a dozen eggs into a bowl. I remembered him stumbling the night before like a sleepwalker down Mass Ave. His cartoon, the one knocking into walls with his neon bracelet lit up in the downstairs of the Middle East. Mobb Deep was rapping with that eerie piano, and Seamus had his arm chained around my neck as Gerry parted through the crowd, grinning at us like he'd just smoked meth. Seamus shoved him back into the swarm.

Later, Seamus drove us to this dive close to home as we chugged road sodas. Seamus and I got in, even with my fake. We left Gerry to get booted out front. He was saying, "Wait, wait, wait," to the bouncer.

The first couple photos I ever took were these ones of Gerard, back when Seamus and I first started, in the fall when my Intrepid kicked it and Seamus fixed it at his shop free of charge. I sat on the foldout chair holding a cup of grainy black coffee as he wiped oil from his hands with a rag and fucked me with his eyes.

Gerry was parked in the garage, passed out in the back seat of his Buick, his construction boots chalked with dirt. I tacked it on the corkboard but got better at printing. Seamy smiling at me, six foot five and dimpled, a pool cue resting in his fist, the billiards lamp throwing a circular glare around his crotch.

"Didn't know orbs could give dome," Seamus said when I showed him. Then he cracked a beer, drained it, and crushed the can in his fist. I wanted him to see the tone, this swampy green that I didn't have to explain in class because I never handed it in. In the photo, Seamy's chin is up, he's saying something as I snapped, Gerry draped across his shoulder. Gerry's eyes are closed and it looked like he was sleeping, but I knew he wasn't. He was listening to Seamus's every word.

Seamus went for a smoke and left the door wide open. Gerry flipped over as the cold rushed in and said, "Aiy! I'm not leaving," in his sleep.

I zipped up one of Seamus's hoodies, then reached my hand down the drain, past piled-up dishes in the shallow gray water. I pulled up a soggy pizza crust and half a chicken bone. I looked up to see him in the kitchen window. He unzipped the hoodie and slid his hand up the jersey to flick my nipple. The coffee stopped sputtering and I unscrewed a bottle of Baileys.

"It's a holiday, baby!" Seamus said, digging for Coronas in the fridge.

Gerry joined us in consciousness. He'd transformed the *Cape Cod* blanket into a shawl and slumped over the table. The deep shadows under his eyes looked like party-store makeup.

"How long you been dead?" Seamus said.

"I'm trying to f-fackin wake up." Gerry had a stoner's stutter, a statie's severe buzz, and very bad breath, like gunk flicked from floss.

"Gerry," I said. "The fuckin' F-word is not a comma."

"Do you see this kid?" Seamus said. "He's not a ghost?"

"I said *fack* you," Gerry said, Boston ingrained and gravelly in his throat. The caps of cans when they spin on bar tops.

"You need some hand sanitizer, kid. What's wrong with you?"

"It's w-wicked freezing," Gerry said, then stared into his mug with this stricken look.

"Then why don't you go home?" I said.

"Shut the fuck up, Nat. W-why aren't you in school?"

"We're seeing a movie tonight," I said. Gerry nodded. "The last showing's at nine forty-five."

I looked at Seamus. He looked at Gerry.

To Seamus by way of Gerry, I said, "You got plans?"

He forked eggs into his face. "Yeah, I plan on s-stopping it," he said.

Seamus leaned across the table and whipped the blanket off Gerry. Gerry curled, that spaz, his skinny limbs pimpled in the freeze. The burn on his chest gleamed from beneath his throat. Hot coffee when he was a little boy. The burn was the size of a beer can, smooth and pink as bubble gum.

Seamus and Gerard grew up on the same street in Lynn. Lynn, Lynn, city of sin. You don't come out the way you came in. They rode bikes to their first job packing groceries at Shaw's. Got jobs sliding under cars at Valvoline. At least that's what Seamus told me on our first date. Huge hands darkened from oil. Scally cap making a shadow down his throat, where a cross hung gold and delicate. He had me up on a barstool, a pitcher between us because it was a school night. Then Gerry between us with the outline of a fifth in his pocket, trying to fish a cooler beer from over the counter.

We were a threesome. It felt like that, or if Gerry and I completed each other we'd be everything Seamus ever needed. Us cruising into Jerry Remy's late night on either side of Seamus. Gerry snorting salt and squeezing lime juice in his eye before ripping shots of Cuervo. Seamus and I taking over the dance floor. Dripping off Seamus as he swung me, bent my body back so my ponytail dusted the floor, lifted my hips so our lips met.

In the kitchen, Seamus tilted back on the chair, then pulled his hoodie up over his eyes. I let out this brassy sigh, then picked the blanket off the floor. I halved it, went to drape it over the back of the couch but got this edge. I pulled it tight between my fists then lashed it at Gerry's head so it thwacked against his cheek. He jerked back, held his hands in front of his face like a blind man.

In October, the three of us drove out to Salem. I skipped school. We drank Cuddy's on Seamus's stoop, watching the sun light up the leaves on the walk. Seamus raced the length of the pike with a wrist on the wheel and I rode shotgun, Gerard like our kid in the back seat.

We parked crooked and walked toward the shore, passing the last of the liter. The sun off the water scorched through my hair. Maybe I was drunk, but I thought I could feel the dead all around me, that I could connect with them. I half read *The Crucible* for English and fancied us characters. The ones stumbling on the cobblestone, heading towards the wilderness.

I had a list in my jeans of all these places I wanted to see: the Witch Trials Memorial, Pickering Wharf, some walking tour. But we couldn't walk. Next thing we were in a tourists' bar with a gold-plated ceiling, stone walls, and candles. We sat and drank for hours, my hair twisted into dreads from the wind and salt. Gerry wrote incoherent diatribes to me with his eyes.

"Y-ya know who you look like," Gerry said, slugging his bottle by the neck. "Medusa."

"Take another shot," I said.

"B-bartender," Gerry said to nobody. The cold focus in his eyes drained pink and sensitive.

"Take another shot, Gerry," I said.

His eyes mutated, turning to something skittering and silvery as beetles. Gerry pounded his fist on the table, and it was enough to slosh over my beer.

"Burn her at the stake!" he shouted.

I jumped off my stool to blot the beer from my chest.

"B-burn her at the stake," he said as the stool shot from between his legs and he crashed to the floor with it, grasping the stool like a lover.

I swung to look at Seamus, but he was laughing so hard he was noiseless. Gerry tossed the stool at the bar and it split in one crack. He wound his legs across the floor like a broken clock in a nightmare. Seamus had these slits in his eyes like it was the best thing he'd ever seen. I don't remember the rest. Seamus said we went on a Ferris wheel and I guess I remember the view. It was spectacular, colors upon colors, neon splitting the sun above the century-old buildings. Seamus said I dropped my purse at the top to measure the fall. I tried to jump out and when Seamus held me down, I cried like a child.

By the afternoon, I'd given up on the movie. I was back to the dishes, scraping crust from a pan and rinsing our plates. Seamus and Gerry were kicked back in the living room, laughing maniacally at the way the officer in *Beverly Hills Cop* said "banana." Gerry flicked a bottle cap at Seamus. Seamus flicked one back, harder, Gerry with his elbows up by his face.

I was in a rare state of peace, and went at the rust around the faucets. Grease came up easy on the countertops, but the floor was my favorite. Something about being on hands and knees, getting all around the edges, between the tiles and the grout. Puffy paper towels coming back torn and black. I threw them away and the trash built up, cheeseburger wrappers and empty bottles stuffed into thirty racks. I made it go on forever, the whole kitchen smelling like black licorice, using my nail to scratch away a single spot on the linoleum, a violin solo going by my ear.

By the time it got dark, I was spent. I straightened out unpaid bills on the counter, sipped my beer, and emptied the silverware drawer.

"Get over here," Seamus said, swinging his arm lazily off the back of the couch.

"First of all," I said.

"Second of all," Seamus said.

I slid next to him on the ash-stained couch. *MTV Jams* was on and he got up to blare it. He held out the remote, squinting with his beer to his heart. The last of the sun spilled onto the carpet from the sliding doors where Seamus once pitched a propane tank off the balcony. Beyond it, the sun flattened over the rooftops of the triple-deckers. I leaned forward, cracked another beer. Seamus swung back as it hissed, looked at me like I said something.

"Shhhhh," he said, holding his finger to his lips. "You just gotta shut up."

I stared at him as I tilted my can. Warm beer dripped down the sides of my chin. Before I could set it down, he was throwing me over his shoulder, slapping my butt.

"Idiots," Gerry muttered.

I held on to his neck as Seamus spun me, all the blood gushing to my scalp, straining my face. I hung on but he dropped me back onto the couch, flipped me to slap my ass once more. A car rushed by and the headlights swept over the ceiling. Gerry and I watched Seamus step back to comb his fingers through his hair. He took his arms over his head to pull off his shirt.

I stood and held up my palms. Seamus held up his, the tips of his fingers beating mine by an inch. We laced up. Seamus tightened his grip and wound me onto the carpet like I was being arrested in slow motion. He locked my wrists against the floor. I took in the sharp scent of rubber, my cheek next to Gerry's construction boots. More cars rushed past. The light made the ceiling ripple like the waves oil makes in a puddle.

The music from the TV slowed. R&B hour and "Nobody's Supposed to Be Here" started playing. Seamus let go of my wrists. I flipped him over and nailed his chest to the floor. I straddled his waist, bent to kiss him, but he jerked up his hips to lift mine with his till we were suspended like two ice-skaters.

Gerry stayed relaxed on the couch with an arm up under his head as we held the pose. Then, like a spark from an outlet, Seamus flipped me under him. We wrestled like brothers in a struggle, pinning each other and grunting. Gerry sipped his beer, his eyes trained on me from above. I heard my head thwack back onto the coffee table. Seamus propped my neck up.

I took advantage and punched at his chest, but there was no point.

He tugged off my shirt in a flourish. I held up my arms as my back glided over the carpet, my spine a string of fire as he dragged me. His chest an apparition of sweat. Gold cross swinging across his chest, naked Jesus small enough to swallow. When Seamus stood still above me, Jesus glowed bronze, his ankles restrained and crossed.

"You're a loser," I said, watching for a twitch in the corner of Seamus's lip, a spasm from the purple vein in his shoulder.

Seamus spat into his palm, then slapped me and pushed my cheek down against the carpet. He yanked down my jeans, then pulled up my hips so my ass grazed his crotch. I glanced up at Gerry. Gerry was part of this. Seamus shoved my head down again and I flooded with heat, same way as when we came home late and Seamus left the bedroom door open. Gerry standing there in the doorway with his beer as Seamus grabbed at my tits from behind.

Once in a while I felt bad for Gerard. A couple months back he was sweet on this girl. He invited her to the bar to watch the Pats play on a Sunday. He showed up all suave, his hair gelled in a fresh lineup, though his dandruff dried in clumps. He was decked out in a collared shirt, sitting with his knee shaking on the stool, clearing his throat between slow sips of Guinness. He ordered another, tried, but couldn't pace it as he had with the first.

And the equation multiplied. The chick never showed. Seamus told him to fuck her, she probably sucked cock for quarters. But Gerard wouldn't say anything about her, not a word. I placed my hand on his shoulder on instinct, rubbed his back a little, but couldn't breathe when his head dropped onto my neck. It shocked me, but I kept his head there. Seamus screamed at the screen, then accused us of being gay for each other during commercials. Gerry stayed mum through the win, then stuck the wrong end of a cigarette between his lips. He limped to the door, rammed his shoulder into it, then stumbled back. The bartender shot me a death stare, so I got up.

"I j-just," he said, slurring, "I hate doors."

"I can see that," I said, and pushed the heavy door against the wind as he flew out into the street with his palms up against headlights that swerved past him.

Seamus ran his hands up my torso, then unclipped the back of my bra, tossed it over Gerry's face. Gerry brought his beer to his lips between the straps. Seamus's hands on my neck reeked of gasoline. He hooked them over my throat, then ran his fingers up the back of my scalp as they caught in my hair. He scrunched a fistful to get my head back. I let my jaw hang open so Gerry could see the gleaming curds of my sparkling pink throat. Gerry put his elbows on his knees.

During Thanksgiving break, Gerry and I stood in the front yard of Seamus's mom's house sipping French vanillas while Seamus packed up her piece-of-shit Victorian. Gerry had paid for my coffee. I hated him because he was a foul human being with a nightmare existence, but times like that, both of us standing around, waiting for Seamus to do something, I did love him.

Seamus stuck his head out the third-floor attic window with an old Sony TV in his arms. I can still see him, big arms around the box as the TV edged its way out. It dropped from the sky, pieces scattering like electrical fire on the walk. I took out my camera to take a shot, all the busted chips and green wires splayed like guts. I called it something dramatic, like "Broken City," and tacked it up on the corkboard. I hadn't been back to class since.

On the carpet, teeth turned crooked in my stomach. Sweat pooled in the small of my back. Seamus blocked my scrappy left hook. The teeth flared, numbed. I went slack as Seamus fucked me like the world was ending. One time I had blacked out on the carpet like this. It was late night and Gerry was nodding out on the recliner. Seamus brags to this day, to anyone he can tell, that it was the best sex he's ever had. It wasn't the first time I had to take the morning-after pill, but it seemed like the most important.

Seamus swiped my stomach with a rag, then tossed it at Gerry. I wrapped my arms around my shoulders and curled into myself as Seamus stood tall. I sprawled out my arms like wings in the snow. Seamus reached down and slapped my stomach. He stepped back, admired the handprint reddening above my belly button, as Gerry stood up from the couch like it was his turn.

It was his turn.

He looked down on me like he always wanted to, then slid off his tank top. The burn on his throat caught the light, a gleaming pink blur. The burn was alive. It glowed like a halo, crowning his throat. It flashed itself as it came toward me, then winked. I waited, and the waiting made me smile, because I thought I knew what came next. But Gerard didn't hesitate. There was no twitch, second thought, no stutter. He raised his boot above my chest and stomped. Even the carpet heard the crack.

# FRANKIE

# SHELLEY BENEATH US

DRIED BLOOD ON THE wall of our building by the stairs, where Shelly's crouching. The streaks go faint around her head, then drip into exclamation points. She holds a sponge and scrubs as we walk towards her, my thumbs hooked under my backpack. It's heavy with psych textbooks and Serena's old jean jacket with the fur collar she gave me once October hit, when walks to Emmanuel started to freeze through our bones even in the white sun.

Serena walks ahead of me in the hall, then lays her palm on Shelly's heaving back. I look away from Shelly's crying and the blood, rusty as the leaves on our steps. We call Shelly a lady, the downstairs lady, but really, she's only a few years older than us. She lives alone, beneath us in the ground-floor apartment. No cable when we first moved in and Shelly was clunking around beneath us. Every night we'd hear the screech of her faucet.

One time we were taking out the trash. Shelly a slit of flesh through the cracked bathroom window. Stringy hair unwashed like when we comb ours through with coconut oil. She was belting a show tune on the toilet, her knees knocked together. Her nipples bright as zits. Serena does this impression of it, but it's more serious than mine. She fake knits with the chopsticks from our takeout and rocks back and forth. The air still, operatic.

"My dog has cancer," Shelly says. She says it in a whisper, fast, like a cough.

"We know," I say, and can't shake the cold from my voice. She's crouched, rounded back, knees and shoulders pointing forward like a gargoyle. A strand of hair falls straight across Shelly's face. Serena fixes it behind her ear.

"He got out the front," Shelly says. "He's gone!"

"Do you want us to look for him?" Serena says. Her dark eyes water at the faintest hint of feeling. She follows it, pain a highway with fast, conspicuous signs. She skipped three days of work to swing with me in the park when my mom died, knowing she'd be fired.

Later, Serena tilts her head back in the shower. "Shelly's dog's going to kick it soon."

"That dog has malaria up the asshole," I say.

"It's cancer."

"I know that." A stream of white soap pools down her chest, frothing around her DNR tattoo. She taps the razor against the tile, a habit I hate, the suds hardening to scum I can't clean with Clorox.

"Sorry," she says, letting me wash my hair first.

In the kitchen, Serena sprawls on the couch in a bra, her nipple spilling out of the cup. She lights a pine tree candle, then a cigarette from the glow, and dips her finger in the oily puddle of wax. Our coffee table a junkyard of mugs, candles, and remotes. We talk till the Tylenol PMs slow our speech, then fall asleep at four, blanketed as mummies.

When it's bright, I tiptoe in wool socks around the kitchen to start coffee. I set a steaming mug down in front of Serena, her hair splayed as if in midair. I see her smashing bricks through windows in a dream I'm not alive enough to be in. Swimming through shards to save bodies in bathtubs. I slip into her room, glide on one of her lipsticks before my 9 a.m. I pull the stick across my lips, then smack. There's a guy in the front row whose name I don't know, with tan elbows and hair that dips above the back of his neck.

I race down the steps, the frost on the window making diamonds of light on the bloody wall. It's when I'm outside, when I drop my backpack to lock the door, that Shelly's dog surges towards me, paws my chest. He's almost human, his limbs stretched to my shoulders, tongue hanging loose and hot. Blood covering half his face like a ski mask where the tumor at the top of his head had burst.

I lurch back onto the railing, scaling the side, breathing through the pinhole in my lung. The eagerness of his eyes, unaware of his injury. Trained to be called to and held by Shelly. He backs away and stays by the door. The loyal huff of his breath in the cold.

*Fucking dog.* I jump off the side of the railing and sprint. *If I loved you,* I think on the jam-packed train, *I'd have to help you.* I shuffle late into school. The math on the board is my friend. I jot it all down, lulled. I know the chance of it being true is virtually zero, but I think the dog died the moment I saw the striation of my lips in the girls' room mirror. The color drained and dried across my mouth.

# GOOD JOB

MCDONALD'S WAS A LONG time ago. I wore a maroon visor and my cutoff jeans. I was fourteen, then fifteen. The walk was three miles and I did it both ways, after school when the cars from Route 9 blew my hair straight back, then at night when I veered past the broken mattresses below the underpass. I had to wear that visor, which was the only part I hated and maybe the smell that fused with my sweat, a mop soaked in sewer water.

It was my job to take out the trash at the end of the night. Hot puddles of chocolate milk gurgled on the asphalt as I hauled the sopping bags over the fence. Trash juice ran down my legs and pooled through my sneakers, still damp from the last shift.

My first paycheck I cashed at the supermarket and left half for my mom in the bread box. I made six dollars an hour, and with my first raise five cents more, but half that was something to her. Our manager Glen let us store liters in the walk-in fridge, and when Serena came, I slid her trays of french fries when he faced the highway in the corner booth, sulking with his Sprite. I made a point to tell Serena that I wasn't about to eat dinner off the dollar menu for the rest of time.

One job was community service, so I didn't get paid. September of sophomore year, Raffa and I were caught in a car trashed with empty cans and unprescribed bottles of oxy littered under the floor mats. Benny was driving but barely. Maria was a Mexican woman who ran the Salvation Army. Tuesday nights the trucks came to unload trash bags filled with gemstone rings, jean jackets, Sega games, and paperbacks.

Before I stocked shelves, she let me sort the junk on a foldout table and pick the VHS tapes I wanted to keep. She let me pull my arms through jean jackets, and she'd clap at me in the mirror. On the ends of the shelves were hairy lollipops, cold pennies, and tarnished quarters. I kept all the change and dumped my mason jar at the Coinstar, closed my eyes as the change rattled through the slot. I'd guess the total, shoot low so I'd feel rich, then watch the screen light up like a video game with all those cherries and diamonds spinning and flashing.

I took the slip up front and had enough to pierce my lip. Maria was the only one to notice. She called me Frankie baby, *lindo, conejito*. When there were no customers, she showed me Kodaks of her babies in Mexico. She'd drive me all the way home, her plastic rosary clattering around the rearview mirror. Most nights I'd find my mom snoring on the kitchen floor, arms clasped overhead like a diver, her drowned breathing a broken radiator.

At Ernesto's, the oversized white tee with the doughboy logo was a downgrade, but I could tie the extra fabric with a loose rubber band. I also learned how to swear in Greek and stretch pizzas that, despite my best intentions, melted into the distinct shapes of hearts. I then had to deliver them down Comm Ave in my mom's rickety Jeep, which I started with a butter knife. One time Brendon LaMarre, the guy whose neck I stared at for two grades straight, swung open the door to his brownstone in his own band's T-shirt.

"Nice shirt," he said, snorting.

"You too," I said, and wanted to hurl the steaming box into his garbage by the curb. I zoomed off and circled the Shaw's parking lot listening to the whole Radiohead album before I went back to pick up the next batch of orders.

In the summer, the lady who ran the restaurant at the golf course showed me how to drive the beer cart steady over bumps.

"Do not, and I mean do not, drive fast," she said, her sunglasses on the top of her head. "You will tip this thing right into the swamp."

In the kitchen I counted change, my back an hourglass of sweat, as she overflowed a teaspoon, then whipped up muffin batter with her eyelashes theatrically low, like I wasn't what she was measuring.

The course was green as postcards, and I'd pop the cooler on the sides of the cart, a treasure chest of silver cans, three bucks each. A man in a pink polo, his temples beaded as the can in his fist, would tilt the beer back while I sorted through the ice, his eyes on the drawstring of my shorts.

The next summer I drove the cart like a maniac, tearing off into the woods while grown men waved clubs in the air, the tailpipe of the cart dripping gasoline. The branches in the woods made shadows of lace on the pages of the books I found in my attic—mysteries, the edges cornered. I wondered what my mom had been thinking when she read those same words.

Sometimes Serena would meet me, her skinny legs hiking up the path. I'd toss her a beer. Then we'd swerve back down to the course, and with Serena hanging onto the seat next to me, I felt giddy and protected, and charged five dollars a beer. There were grass stains on the men's golf shoes when they plucked out bills from their leather wallets. I looked them dead in the eye when I handed them their ice-cold Coors Lights, said thank-you with my lips wide and pink. I was careful about the counting. I marked the beers and left exact change, to the cent, in an envelope at the end of the day. I'd store the extra cash under the pull-out register and count the stack when I parked the cart in the shed. I tucked the twenties into my bra. The way I figured it, what were two extra bucks to a hundred well-off men when two hundred was a Christmas morning for my mom? I didn't get fired right away.

I cashed checks at Shaw's. I'd leave my mom big bills and odd change in the bread box. I'd come back with groceries, too, cream cheese, rotini, Toaster Strudels. One time I bought a whole rotisserie chicken, just for me, just once, and ate it on the bench by the mini carousel, pried it apart, peeled off the glistening skin, and dangled it onto my tongue.

I didn't buy nail polish or tampons or thick magazines. I bought gas for the Jeep, most times in quarters. I stopped filling the tank all the way when I found red Solo cups of warm chardonnay in the cup holders. I bought white paint at Ace when she asked me to sand the rotting back porch and fix the color. I poured the paint into an aluminum tray. It guzzled out in the heat and smelled like cat pee. The tarp on the aboveground pool was torn and held down by concrete bricks but it flapped uncontrollably, so I yelled for my mom to repeat herself. She stood behind the screen door, cigarette up by her ear, the smoke twisting a gray wreath around her eyes.

"You're doing a good job."

I worked at Staples and the lights made the insides of my eyes look like an Etch A Sketch when I shut them, my fingers pressed to my temples. One time I got a call and had to ask my manager Linda to drive me to the bank and then to the police station in West Roxbury during our lunch break. A third DUI meant I had to take the rest of the money from my savings. I signed a clipboard and waited. On her way home, my mom talked to Linda about mousse versus gel and discounts for printers at Staples.

After that I was told I could stay at the register, rearranging pens. I wrote things down on the loose sheets of office paper that circulated in the back rooms. I'd ring up a customer real quick, hand them the plastic bag and receipt with a genuine smile. Then I'd tilt my head to jot down estimates. By that time, calculating my earnings felt like loosening the cement that was drying inside me. I was sixteen but had skipped a grade. College was coming. I did basic math. It would take four months of six-hour shifts at Staples. If I took out an eighty-thousand-dollar loan, I'd be fifty-seven and a half by the time I could pay it all back. Other times I tried to write what I was thinking, but it was harder.

I needed a side job. I saw a flyer tacked to a phone pole and started to babysit for a one-year-old down the street. Emma nestled into my arm to take bottles, her eyes shut with trust. She tottered around the carpet, falling to her knees. She waved her hands for me to pick her up, and I would rock her into my chest, not letting go, even when she kicked.

Emma's dad insisted on driving me home. I climbed into his tall SUV and he drove the four blocks slowly, then pulled over into the back parking lot before Comella's. I tried to mistake the AC for his breathing. I stared at the teeth-whitening billboard across the street, but he slid his pants down to the pedals.

"Will you suck it?" he said.

I bent above his lap and he jerked his hand down my neck, then crammed my throat with his cock, which tasted like used Band-Aids. Outside I heard a breeze, the bird's frantic reporting, my ears warm and chirping. My sour spit slicked down him in white strings. As he started to cry, he came.

"Oh my god," he said. "Oh my god."

He covered himself and put his forehead on the wheel. I wanted to kill him.

"It's okay," I said, looking back at the billboard. "Don't worry."

I worked at the grocery store pulling spoils. Cardboard boxes of rotten bananas weighed more than I did, but I'd wheel them away with the dexterity of a gymnast. I kept an X-Acto knife hooked to my side like a cop. I would slice empty boxes apart like they were faces I hated. They let me wear headphones and I'd zone out hard, hiding gum under my tongue for hours at a time. Yogurt was my favorite to stack. I'd kneel on the other side of the fridge with the cold boxes, the garage door open so the outside world looked green and remote. Six-packs of plastic felt cool on my fingertips, and I loved to get them perfect. On my lunch break I swiped a yogurt from the spoils bin—usually only the top was busted. I sat on the church steps and licked the inside of the lid while a Catholic Mass filtered out, women's heels clacking past me, varicose veins flashing through flesh-colored tights.

I'd know before I walked home that my mom had peed her pants on the couch. Midnight, and I'd help her step into a new pair of underwear in the living room. Oversized bottles of Carlo Rossi would be spread aimlessly across the coffee table like giant jugs of piss. She'd tip over, her thighs glowing in the darkness as she kicked her legs into the air, screaming generalities at a person who wasn't there: "Not this time, motherfucker," or "You knew it. Everybody was." She'd tire of herself. She'd take her knees up to her chest on the carpet in one final heave. I'd get her up and she'd steady her palm on my back as I slid her pants up one leg at a time. If she'd stumble, I'd think of choking her with them, the fabric wrung around her neck. Instead I whispered, "Good job," or "Come on."

I chopped onions and never cried. I did dishes, my sleeves rolled up past my sunburn, my wrists bumping against floating steak knives while the froth disappeared down the drain. Behind the bar I inhaled the buttery sting when I poured chardonnay. I climbed ladders to hoist the long ends of mops horizontally across a gray movie screen. You can't imagine the dust, the accumulation of human hair. I was so small against the screen, the size of an ear.

I counted drawers, came to prefer numbers to words, the lull of exacting. I often checked my savings, swiping my card outside the vestibule to contemplate the tiny green digits. I filled out my FAFSA and waited for my mom to just sign the last page. I left it on the counter. I kept saving. I waited.

# SERENA

# TROUBLE

WE WERE ALL THE same age, our new neighbors and us. Our puppies were the same age, our new puppy and their new puppy. We learned this as the neighbors hauled boxes out of their car and our little prize thrashed his neck against the thick leash we'd bought at Petco. Unleashed, he ran in viciously fast circles or mistook my ankles for chew toys. He found my cigarettes, even when I hid them, and ripped them to bits. *We should call him Ashtray*, I thought.

"That's why we buy him toys, dumbass," Niko said. I didn't know this. I didn't know much. Cigarettes were already overpriced, and like a homeless person, I was picking through the promising ones.

Outside the new neighbors' car, for a split second, we expected that we could become great friends. The neighbors and us, just like normal couples. Just like the puppies, normal puppies, who were pawing at each other like lovers.

"What's your puppy's name? Sorry I'm eating strawberries," the girl said. She dropped the carton on the grass, the strawberries rolling next to her laundry basket. The puppies teamed up to demolish the berries, then chewed her sweatshirt collar, the gray sleeve darkening with slobber.

"His name's Trouble," I said. News to Niko, who looked at our puppy reluctantly, but I had him there. It wasn't something he could argue with. Our puppy had hole-punching teeth and coal-lined eyes like an emo teenager.

"Get back," I said. Trouble was spread eagle on the concrete as the neighbors' puppy tongued his privates. I jerked his leash back. Not on my watch. I scooped up Trouble as he writhed in my arms, then started yelping like a Mormon girl during a kidnapping. I edged up the stairs while Niko charmed the neighbors. The girl bought it, and started talking his head off about how we should all go to dinner. Or make it.

"We should have a dinner party," the girl said. "We're twenty-six. We're over partying."

Briefly I saw myself from the view of the light fixture on the stairs, head-first, knocked out, the door locked, bolted, my credit cards strewn below me like clues.

Later, while Trouble raised his leg to pee freely in the corner of the kitchen, I asked Niko if he noticed that both the girl and the guy neighbors had lazy eyes. Before I asked him this, I prefaced by saying that it wasn't the reason I disliked them both individually and as a couple. I just thought, what were the chances? Both of their eyes milked at the center, identically, their pupils going googly like Magic 8 Balls.

Trouble panted with his tongue out. I mirrored him, my tongue out in what I imagined was a parched look, while I waited for Niko to say something. I squeezed Trouble like a tube until he slinkyed out of my grip.

"What does it matter about their eyes?" Niko said, pouring bacon grease into a beer can. *It matters to me*, I thought. Did they look at each other, or half look at each other, and think, *You complete me*?

I hid under the dining room table with Trouble, taking the padded tips of his paws against my fingers. I loved Trouble so much that I kind of wanted to hurt him. I ran my fingers down the tender muscles of his underside and bit longingly at the aching inside of my cheek. Trouble stared back like he was so miserably disappointed in me, to the core, though he'd only known me a month. He freed himself from the cage of my arms. He gagged, hunched, and heaved onto the hardwood. My cigarettes.

"No! Trouble! No!" I said. I pointed my finger to emphasize my anger, but it reworded itself as excitement. "Go! Trouble! Go!"

I slid down the wall with my head in my hands as Trouble ran track around the table. I thought of my brother when he was little and couldn't speak. How he twisted his hands in front of his mouth to talk to our mom. Blowing her kisses, pointing to cookies in the aisle, then back to his mouth. Mouth to object, object to mouth. His sincere words dribbling out like applesauce. Since I couldn't understand him, I would push him as hard as I could when no one was looking. I'd push him again, his helplessness the maker of my fury.

Trouble howled, barks like gunshots, his paws slipping and clicking on the hardwood.

"Why are you such a fucking baby?" Niko said, walking past with a plate of stacked bacon, paleo fanatic that he was. Niko was gorgeous—everyone knew. He had slick black hair and tan skin like a man on the beach whose shoulder beads with water. Our children would be blended. I sometimes imagined their sparkling cheeks and kinky, highlighted hair. They would be him with my affectations. In photos, their eyes tiny riots, wild with inarticulate demands.

I want to tell you why I disliked our neighbors, the girl in particular, so you won't hate me as much as my puppy hated me. The following week on the back stairs, the girl remarked on the convenience of our shared lawn out back. When she spoke, I couldn't tell which eye to look into, so I looked at the lazy one. It swung up, receiving radio signals. There was a weird comfort in this. I had the advantage of feigning interest openly, the disfigurement like an invitation where only your true self is welcome to the party.

"There's going to be a lot of shit in that yard," the girl said, like a fact. Maybe I didn't know things, like why Trouble needed monthly shots when I didn't have health care, or why he required wet food, a spoonful, mixed into a cup of dry food when you could just do either, but I knew damn well that we should clean up after him. We were adults. Every day, we were adults.

Upstairs in our kitchen, Trouble would start barking, and Niko and I would freeze. His barks were an alarm going off that we did not know how to disassemble.

"What do you want?" Niko would say. "Huh?"

Trouble would hop madly at my waist. "You think I'm playing, esé? Say something."

Niko would step towards me. He'd say, "Why didn't you set her straight?"

I'd jerk my head back without meaning to. Niko had hit me many times. More than many. More than hit. Smashed my face into the wall where a mirror from a garage sale hung by the door where I never failed to check my gaze.

A month later, I stood on the lawn, shaking my knee. The sky was bleeding down the center like a gunshot wound. I was waiting for Trouble to go already so I could clomp back upstairs to watch Bravo and eat Doritos standing up. He would circle me, the Doritos a bag of crack. His tongue hanging loosely, that deranged shark. It was among these thoughts that I noticed a piece of shit on the lawn.

"Do I have to do everything?" Niko said, all smug, like he was the smarter one. We were on our deck with the higher view of downtown. I'd forgotten to take out the trash.

*School is a job,* I thought.

"'Cause you can't do anything," Niko said. The twelve-pack of craft beers he'd drunk stunk from the sweat that ridged his bald chest, which was now up against my chin.

After I reset my nose with a pencil, I went to be alone in our guest room, where Niko's electric guitars hung on the wall like a rich kid's toys. I hid in the closet. I was the guest, to talk to the guy I'd been talking to. When he teased me, I teased back, my old clogs smelling like burnt rubber.

The day after the Fourth, both in our pajamas, the girl and I stood on the lawn as our puppies rocketed towards each other, tumbling together like free-fallers. It was noon and I'd already had two Coronas. My right eye was a puff pastry enclosing a pink slit. Niko had taken my freshly inked arm the night before, squeezing out a code to what awaited me at home. I wanted to be alone. Really alone. Before Niko, before Trouble, the neighbors, before I could even remember. I wanted to be alone with the guy I wasn't supposed to be talking to. I'd go anywhere with him.

"Trouble got bigger," the girl said.

My heart sprang like a punch from an arcade game. I couldn't measure change with what was mine. But he wasn't mine; I'd never asked for Trouble. Niko and I had woken up from a bad fight. A purple shiner covered my eyelid in a deep swell but matched my makeup, so we decided to go for a walk. We were walking past the thick window of a shelter. Niko thought Trouble could be a gift, a romantic gesture. *Wow,* I thought, *I've never received a gift I'd have to walk for fifteen years.*

When he picked Trouble out of the litter, I thought he'd stay that same size forever, the size of an organ, sticky-soft and warm. We took Trouble home. He trembled, then ripped up the sectional Niko had bought without insurance.

"Cut it out, you fucking monster!" I screamed.

In my spot, in the closet of the guest room, he fell asleep in my arms, where he had puppy dreams. His paws moved like levers in a field where he was free and unleashed.

The neighbor dog nipped at Trouble's neck. The girl and I watched as they tugged at each other's skin, then retreated, their eyes fixed intently on the other's, waiting to pummel. I didn't care about my eye. I was too tired to dab it with concealer and set it with powder. I wanted her to see.

"They like each other," the girl said. I knew what she meant. She meant us. She wanted us to like each other. She wanted it since that first day they pulled up with their goddamn sorcerer's auras and dirty laundry.

"Stop it," I said to Trouble.

"Do you want to go to that new Mexican place down the street? As couples?" she said.

I opened my mouth, but the heat crawled in and thickened my tongue. I wanted to go, I did. I wanted to sit next to her in the booth with my superior eyes, tracing my fingers down the row of similar but different margaritas. She was waiting, with her permanent grin on, I could tell, though I stayed busy watching Trouble.

He was lunging this way and that way, trapped in the yard, thinking he was free. Was he bigger and why couldn't I tell? When would I know? And then the dogs started barking, cruel little yips, and I grabbed at the leash, but Trouble had this new kind of force as he lunged at the neighbor dog. I looked at the girl, thinking she would do something. But for the first time she said nothing. Dumb chick just stood there, waiting. I was wordless, wanting. Wanting to look where she looked, but she was looking at me.

# SADIE ESCOBAR

MARIAH HAD BEEN STRAIGHTENING her hair the first time I showed up to babysit. She opened the door in maroon scrubs, and when she went to hug me, I felt the heat from the iron transfer to my cheek.

"Hey, babe," she said. "Come see the babe."

She took my wrist through the discount-candle-scented living room, past a flat-screen, hundreds of DVDs spread across a bookshelf. TV series in boxes stretching like accordions, romantic comedies, R&B concerts, aerobics videos. At that time, I not so secretly despised assholes who worshipped books like *The Fountainhead*, any jackoff intellectual's wet dream. You could say I admired the sincerity of her collection.

I followed Mariah up to Sadie's room, dimmed by a thick pink blanket tacked over the window to drown out the sounds of the beeping garbage trucks or the downstairs neighbors who leaned off the deck with Solo cups. Deep in her crib, Sadie was obscured, her fists covering her face.

"I love to wake her up," Mariah whispered, her lash line rimmed with white glue that gave her eyes an unnatural intensity. She scooped her out and instantly set her in my arms. She watched as Sadie twisted, opening her eyes, glossy with the complicated look of being held by a stranger upon waking.

I walked to babysitting from Jimmy's place in Fenway. Three miles in the heat down Comm Ave, past brownstones that sat like gingerbread houses. The gardens were trimmed with the look of military crew cuts, a cotton-candy smell rising from the hypergreen grass. I'd walk the Common through Downtown Crossing, hopscotching junkies who slept on the cobblestone under the shade of Payless awnings. Towards the harbor, gray skirts and ties flitted into buildings, and it was salty and cool by the waterfront bars where stools were flipped over tables.

Christian and Mariah lived in Southie before Southie realized it was on the water and big signs for luxury condos appeared by the T, driving out the scally-capped Irish townies and their opposites, college kids in Izod seeking cheaper rent. Their apartment was on the top floor of a triple-decker on a lettered block, which meant I learned to clutch Sadie in one arm and haul her stroller in the other, a move that slimmed my hips.

My mentality was that of a soldier. I was never once late, and I didn't complain when other people were. Straightaway Christian took advantage and came rushing through the door three hours past five, a water-fight of sweat on his collared shirt. He'd insist on paying for my cab home. I knew it was to shut me up, so I wouldn't say anything to Mariah, which I didn't.

Christian's black hair was perfectly faded on each side. He wore aviators no matter what and carried the waft of fresh sneakers through the door. He sold time-shares to lonely victims at the Prudential mall. He was a liar. An attorney's letter left folded on the Formica revealed that he owed upwards of twenty-five thousand dollars to a debt collector. This coupled with a video I came across on his laptop of him speedily jerking himself off into a T-shirt, his jaw slack to the camera, confirmed he was a cheater. I had no desire to, but I had to watch until he came. I watched and I watched.

"They're taking advantage of you," Jimmy said.

"What'd you say?" My mind was always elsewhere, feeling around for words. Brady panted between us, then lowered himself down, resting his chin on crossed paws. Jimmy caught his breath, hocking spit into a grassy patch by the Charles. Fifty-one had snuck up on him. We were running but not fucking. Jimmy wore a faded Rangers hat at all times, and beneath it his chest was steady as an ox. For being so broad, I liked his contained nature, his belly, and tried to pin his weight on top of me.

"Took you long enough to get your degree," he said. "Use it."

I listened to his advice but didn't take it. I guess being taken advantage of was okay with me. It meant I didn't owe anyone anything. It meant I was earning something other than money, though I couldn't say what.

A month in and Sadie was rolling over but couldn't yet talk. I liked the way she needed me, that when she cried, it always meant something. On a park bench off D Street I fed her bottles of milk warmed by sunlight. She'd stare at me as she sucked, senselessly blinking. With no warning, she dropped the bottle and reached for my neck. So much of being a mother was coping with the long spans of boredom that were punctuated by seconds of ache so pure they could shatter your rib cage if you weren't breathing right. I wasn't. My ribs felt held by staples.

On the beach, seagulls picked at the tough rings of six-packs. A woman in black spandex passed us with water bottles like suitcases in her grip. She was jogging, but even as she was part blur, I caught the blaze of emotion on her face, her tongue in her teeth, the grit pornographic. She was made of liquid, propelled by the power from inside her.

Sadie had to learn. Her fingers pointed to the tops of trees whose leaves spun light, disco ball refractions across her forehead. Everything was new to her as an acid trip.

"Sadie, look! The sky," I said. *"See the sky."*

She babbled, sounds that verged on words curled and wound like rings of smoke off her tongue. Mariah loved that I took her outside. She told me their previous babysitter, an ex-friend, had taken naps on the couch, leaving Sadie in the crib, and had mistakenly eaten their cat food under the assumption it was cereal. She said I was their angel. A lifesaver. She relayed information in emojis, streams of hearts and trophies and yellow faces switching expressions. She was less of a woman and more of a girl. I saw in a birthday card, filled with pledges from Christian, *baby*s and *please*s, that she was twenty-six, a year younger than me, though I had told her I was twenty and she believed it.

One night Mariah got home before Christian. She watched me reach down towards Sadie, who lay flat-backed, surrounded by plastic light-up toys, on an outstretched blanket. I poked her stomach for that tender baby laugh, all gums and lungs. The front door's bronze handle gleamed from the corner of my eye, but Mariah took me back to Sadie's room and held up the new clothes she'd bought. Hideous polka-dotted headbands, though Sadie was bald. Strappy pink sandals, a single golden rose on the toe, though she couldn't walk.

"I love it," I said, patting a folded two-piece swimsuit. She shuffled through Kodaks she'd printed, Sadie in nothing but a string of pearls and a diaper, propped upright by an oversized stuffed giraffe. In one photo, she sat chunky and cross-legged, smashing a cake. In another, her finger was slicked with frosting, her tongue ultrapink from sugar. In each, Sadie's eyes followed the lens, open and vulnerable.

"These are beautiful," I said, eyeing Sadie, her head tentative on Mariah's shoulder.

Sadie would no longer sit fixed to me. She was flipping over on the carpet, her head craned up, inching forward with her butt in the air. I ran sprints across the apartment to catch her from tumbling down the stairs. With her shoulders strapped in a high chair, her eyes changed expressions like a student in an acting class. If you took away her pacifier, she would scowl, her forehead a dent. If you slipped a mandarin orange onto her tongue, she would roll her whole head back, batting her eyelashes in pleasure. Sadie's teeth were coming in sharp and round, the size of mints.

"Hey," I'd say, holding up a spoon. *"What is this?"* I drew out vowels as if she could catch them on the other side.

Then I'd abandon the spoon. I would say, "Sadie, say something."

I wanted to know what she would say, uninstructed. Instead, she would deliberately throw things. A piece of pasta slicked with butter, a grape. Then she would scowl at the thing on the floor, maddened by its inability to return.

Sadie had electronic toys and blocks, Mariah's broken iPhone, which she would hold up to her ear in upside-down imitation. She didn't have a single book. I went to Trident on my day off and bought her *The Giving Tree*, *Blueberries for Sal*, *The Secret Garden*.

I got a text one day from Christian as I was stepping off the train: *I just saw you on the C line. Don't think I'm a creep.* That next morning there were three bottles of Charles Shaw uncorked by the sink, and the laundry was strewn across the kitchen counter. Bleached-out towels and socks, a pink bra hooked to a pair of Sadie's fuzzy pajamas. I'd drank since I was thirteen, but for Mariah, starting now was like building a house without any floor plans, with no concrete.

Christian came home late but first. He wrote me a check. Forty dollars was missing. I pictured him at the mall, cornering some mother on the cusp outside Sears, luring her into signing paperwork for a vacation down on the Cape. There would be an indoor pool with a hot tub, a porch with a grill, a view of the waves crashing. No cash up front. Time-shares were like buying cake batter on the dollar rack at the grocery store. A good deal but it was going to fuck up your life.

I didn't confront him about the check, not because he was scary in the way I used to feel my father was scary, the way he would reach out to swipe a full glass of milk off the table if you said something he didn't like, then walk away. I was scared of Christian because he wasn't scary, not overtly. He was the kind of criminal who would use turn signals in a high-speed chase; you couldn't tell if he was stupid or nice. Each morning he'd ask, the way a computerized secretary greets a patient, how my day was, though it was 7 a.m. Mariah once joked to me that he was a psychopath.

In September, Mariah called to say she wouldn't need me on Tuesday but would I go spray-tanning with her? Mariah bounced the wheels of the stroller down the steps and we walked through Southie, leaves slashing under the stroller's tires. We talked about Sadie's recent bout of hiccups, how Christian worked six days a week, how they hadn't been out once together since Sadie was born.

"It's on me," she said, bouncing Sadie on her knee. The girl behind the counter waved. "They know us here," Mariah said.

In the spray-tan room, which was less of a room and exactly a closet, I got undressed like I was told and slipped on the black disposable G-string. I stood in front of an aluminum room divider for twenty minutes, waiting for the spray-tan girl to come in and judge the wisps of hair on my nipples, the razor-burn between my thighs. When she did, she kicked up the machine and told me to turn around.

She hosed me with my arms up crucifixion-style, the mist as cold as being stuck in the walk-in freezer at McDonald's.

"You look incredible!" Mariah said when I came out.

I looked like a red pepper and a carrot got in a fistfight. The tan stained my white shirt in patches. At the park, I thought of the way I was turned back to front and doused, how *no* was a word that had been deleted from my genetic code. Mariah and I watched Sadie splash around in the fountain. I wanted to sprint through as the tan ran down my neck and arms, dyeing the kiddie pool a pissy orange.

"Christian and I are splitting up," Mariah said, her mouth tightening.

"That's enough," some mother shouted from the edge, prying her dripping-wet son out by the armpits.

"Oh," I said. I had known Christian was sleeping on the couch. He left his pillow there and never kissed Sadie goodbye. He'd leave and there'd be nothing but the TV in her eyes. I thought of my dad, the smell of basil etched into his fingers.

"Sadie and I need you more than ever," Mariah said. "I want to give you a raise."

"It's a terrible time to talk about money," I said.

"I don't want to make you feel uncomfortable," she said. "I just wanted to be honest with you. You and me, we need each other."

I looked back at her, thinking, *What is this bitch talking about?* She had her sunglasses down to block her expression, so I said, "Totally."

The next week, Mariah asked if I would go to brunch with her.

"This isn't part of your job," Jimmy said, holding his phone to his chest. "Say no."

This was the difference between us, me believing the things I could directly affect were my responsibility, him thinking they were not. He was responsible for a lot. A whole company. He ran PR for festivals and events all over Boston. On weekends, I wore laminated necklaces and drank unlimited vodka while hanging backstage with bands like the Pixies. He owned his place in Fenway above the stadium and I enjoyed the walk-in shower. It wasn't why I was with him. I wanted to say it constantly, like a tic. I insisted on paying him two hundred dollars a month for rent.

"You maintaining your independence?" he'd tease.

At brunch, the stroller got jammed in the doorway. The wait was twenty minutes. I felt Mariah's mood prick. She pushed the stroller back and forth beside the door as a cluster of leggy girls in rompers leaned against the wall with their phones under their noses.

"Shhhh," Mariah hissed as I bent to give Sadie her water. She hurled the heavy plastic bottle between a passing waiter's legs. She screamed like a bird of prey, like she was falling from the sky, like her fingers were being severed one by one.

We were seated an hour later. It was the first time I'd ever really looked at Mariah head-on. She was wearing loads of makeup, winged eyeliner sketched over crow's-feet. Foundation pulled into the corners of the worry lines on her forehead and down under her nose in slash marks.

"It's been a bad week," she said. "I don't mean to bring you into it all."

"You're not," I lied. "I'm here for you and Sadie."

"You have no idea what Christian has put me through," she said. "Your boyfriend is a good guy. I can tell from pictures. How old is he?"

"We kind of met in a weird way," I said.

"He's not a cheater like Christian," she said. "You know that Malcolm Butler jersey, signed and fucking framed on the wall?" I didn't.

"I bought him that. I like to buy gifts that people really appreciate. I just want somebody who will do the same for me."

"You'll find that," I said, regifting sayings. "It takes time."

I thought of Jimmy, his hat pulled down on the rooftop at the Rattlesnake. As if we weren't high enough, I asked him, testing his strength, to lift me up. He held my hips like an ice-skater as my arms helicoptered above the crowd.

"Thank god for you," Mariah said.

The waiter hurried to our table, and I paused as Mariah asked for a mimosa pitcher. The waiter filled our glasses to the top. Sadie struggled to reach over her stroller, then smacked mine to the floor.

"Like mother, like daughter," Mariah said, then kept Sadie's stroller faced to the wall as she wailed. The food came and Mariah looked bleary-eyed when her side of home fries was missing.

"Have some of mine," I said, pushing over my plate.

"I just want to be honest with you. Christian hasn't been home in weeks," she said, knifing ketchup out of the neck. "If he doesn't come home soon, I'm throwing all his shit in the yard."

That night I met Jimmy at Boston Calling. I spotted him threading in and out of the crowd with his headset. When he found me, he brought me a cheeseburger with a basket of french fries.

"Eat the burger first," he said as he took off his Rangers hat.

The Roots were playing "You Got Me" as they crouched and crossed one another on the smoky stage. My phone set off in my pocket and there was no mystery as to who it was. If you could slur through text, Mariah would have been the pioneer. She had seen Christian at a bar with some chick. The security camera caught Mariah punching the girl to the ground. Mariah told me she was arrested, then released.

"That her?" Jimmy said. He held on to the brim of his hat. His assistant, skinny from Adderall, pushed her way towards us with her clipboard, her manic black fly-aways like that of a woman in labor.

"We have to rotate," his assistant said, ignoring me. "Let's go."

"It's like you get off on their shit," Jimmy said, ignoring her, swiping back the hair he had left, then correcting his hat.

"You have no idea what I get off on," I said.

There were times I thought to quit, like the day Mariah ordered a *Date My Mom* onesie. When the wine bottles appeared like knocked-over bowling pins on the kitchen tile. Or even at Starbucks, that first day, when Christian turned around and the baby was strapped to his front, her head bobbing with those ninety-ninth percentile cheeks. Her fat thighs kicking the air. The love I felt for her pulsed with pressure, an overcaffeinated type of love.

After the interview, I dipped behind the gang-signed alley and typed "eighty dollars times three days a week divided by eleven hours a day" into my phone and realized that flat rates were some kind of bullshit. I could make more tonging Munchkins at Dunkin'. I had a friend who used to babysit a kid, and she was paid twenty bucks an hour in undergrad.

I googled: "Swedish word for doing something against instinct?"

I'd quit a lot of things, by that point. I'd left college, then taken night classes, skipped graduation. I'd worked at an after-school program where only the autistic kids handed in papers that made any sense. I worked for Delta, flung myself through cities and terminals, quit. I'd left Niko, the guy who smiled in astonishment, tears filling his eyes after he colored my face with bright bruises. I'd quit my first real job teaching first graders to write three-word sentences: *I have it. This is big. See her go*. Sometimes the simple repetition and those synapses linking was so mysterious that I was left sobbing in the girls' room by the miniature toilets.

I was terrified of bosses. I was set on existing as my own boss. I was terrified of myself.

The next Monday, I took Sadie for an extra-long walk. We stopped in the grocery store and I let her taste a strawberry. Through aisles, she poked her head out of the stroller as if through the window on a road trip, her lips stained a healthy red. I took her to Trident and lifted her on my shoulders so she could trace her finger across the bright spines of autobiographies. At home, she was an overtired brat. She plucked the elastic off the cabinet handle, turned to me with the depraved look of bad-girl hesitancy, then slammed a pot against the wall. She opened DVDs and scratched at the discs as I tugged them back from her. She cried like a maniac in my arms. She slapped at my face.

Later that night, as Jimmy and I sat out on the deck, Mariah texted me photo after photo of Sadie when she was born. Tiny Sadie was unrecognizable, tightly wrapped in cloth with a pimpled, ancient face. Mariah told me she wanted to talk someday about how hard it was to bring a child into the world. Not just the physical pain. It was harder than anything you could imagine, she said. To hold a family together, to be that skin-close to another person. Jimmy and I were splitting a cigarette. We were drinking but we weren't laughing. Below us in the stadium, a bat cracked hard and I felt the home run before I saw its reflection from the flat-screen on the mirror of the glass door.

"Are we losing now?" I asked as he passed back the light.

"Stop talking to her," he said, widening his eyes. "She's crossing the line."

"Why don't you just punch me already?" And I meant it. And Jimmy knew that.

"I won't tell you again," Jimmy said, pulling to the edge of his seat, genuinely hurt. "You're not going to get that here."

When I got to the apartment the next day, Sadie's stroller was flipped over on the stairs, the back wheel turned in on itself like an umbrella whipped up by the wind. At first, I thought Christian had come home, turned his theatrically calm demeanor inside out, but Mariah was in a tank top in the kitchen, her massive boobs spilling out of the lacy cups. Bottles of wine were lined up by height like rows of candles at a night mass. She grabbed one and chugged from the neck. She shut her eyes and wiped her mouth with the back of her palm. A red cut above her lip gleamed with Neosporin.

"I cut myself," she said in a plain voice.

"Looks bad," I whispered, though the look of her in pain excited me. I fingered my ponytail from behind, needing something to touch.

"I'm useless," she said, pouring wine into a water glass.

"You haven't been yourself," I said, though that's exactly who she'd been. "Sadie needs you."

She loaded the dishwasher, scummy knife blades erect, then kicked it shut and leaned against the counter. "Sadie needs both of us, a mom and a dad."

"My dad left," I said. "You call me an angel, right?"

She began to cry, fully, an eyelash coming loose.

"I was fired from the hospital," she said. The other eyelash traversed down her cheek like a centipede. "And by the way, you're twenty-two," she hissed, raising her hand at me. "You don't know anything about what it takes to hold a family together."

"I'm twenty," I corrected. "I'm sorry." I was sorry for a lot of things. Sadie was sleeping—I could hear the whir of the fan from her monitor. "Let's go and see Sadie. We can wake her up."

"I need to lie down." Mariah tripped on her way to the couch. I pulled her up. "I lit a towel on fire last night," she said with a snort, her curvy body sprawled across the couch.

I faked a laugh. "Why?"

"We were fighting in the bathroom."

"About what?" I said, my palms back against the carpet, the way they were when we were watching Sadie run through the fountain.

"He'll never change," she said. I nodded gravely. "We were on this fantasy football team, you know? With all his friends. I texted the entire group saying I'd have to withdraw on account of Christian fucking another chick. Not one of them responded," she said. "How psychotic of them?"

"Totally," I said.

"I had a boyfriend once who hit me. Christian never hit me, but it was worse. He didn't love me."

I stared at my thighs.

"Have you ever wanted to go to Cabo?" she said, seized by the idea, her wet eyes filled with focus.

I picked apart the carpet, mustered, "Not really."

"Good times," she sighed, then rolled off the couch. "Hold on, I want to show you something." She crawled towards me, her cheek close to mine.

"There's this guy," Mariah said. I snuck a glance at her face as she swiped through her phone, something hard rammed under the bags of her eyes. "His name is Robbie," she said with her nail between her teeth. "We were best friends in high school. Missed timing or something."

He was Mariah's type, whatever that meant. She showed me another photo of Robbie in front of a sun-faded baseball field with a small boy on his back.

"That's his son. He's five. Sadie's future older brother?" She cackled, the way nervous people crack during funerals. "He invited me to visit in Rhode Island."

I sat on the edge of her bed as she packed her overnight bag: Victoria's Secret perfume, silky thongs, eyelash glue. She brought me in to wake up Sadie from her nap, but it didn't feel like a job for two. Sadie's head swung back, her hair a dandelion of pink light from the window. A hundred frozen particles. The white bars dividing the room. Light swallowing the carpet.

Sadie didn't have receipts she couldn't find, debt from credit card bills. She hadn't done anything wrong. But when Mariah and I crept in that day, her room was overly warm, sour with the smell of spent diapers and sweat-clung sheets. Mariah lifted her into the air, then palmed her wet head to her chest. Sadie looked at me drowsily. Rhode Island was only a two-hour drive. Mariah said she'd be back the next day.

"You're our angel," she said, and I wasn't sure who she meant as she lifted Sadie higher than the ceiling fan.

I sat with Sadie on the stoop. Her stroller was broken and the refrigerator was empty. I could carry her to the grocery store, or let her down to walk beside me if she didn't run too far ahead. I made a mental list: eggs, bananas, cheddar cheese to melt into Sadie's pasta, passive-aggressive flowers for Mariah.

I watched Sadie descend the stoop backwards. She paused, seeing if I would stop her. Her leggings were bunched around her thighs and I tugged them down. She squatted on the bottom stair, tracing her finger over the gritty bumps on the concrete. My rage was so concentrated that it fused with the sunlight on the dumpster. It made me want to cry, not because Sadie wasn't mine, but because she was Christian's, and where the fuck was he? Sadie said, "Ot"—she meant *hot*, her new favorite word—and I carried her to the store.

I quit. I moved back in with Raffa and got a new job teaching ESL to women who wore high heels with tracksuits. I told Mariah I would find someone else, and even met her at Starbucks for an interview. Some nice girl in school for early childhood education. She had nothing-special hair, a brown suede purse that buckled on the side. She was the one. I listened to Jimmy for once, then I left him. It was too obvious, like a flu passed between us: I was with him because he wouldn't hit me. I left him because he wouldn't hit me.

I went to dirty dives, places like Mary Ann's and Biddy Early's, where I drank from plastic cups and aimed darts at a fuzzy wall. I was back to the hollow buzz of dark jaws trilling broken English into my ear and to milk sugared by cereal in the morning and to the strange comfort of mysterious bruises, my legs shaved and lonely. One night I saw Mariah. It was before close at some waterfront bar when the dancing died and I looked out to the dark lap of the harbor, craving a cigarette, and there she was, sitting on a barstool, wearing a Red Sox hat and tons of lipstick. It was no coincidence, I'd told her to come.

There was a guy behind her, his arm caged around her stool. I tapped his shoulder and he gave me the once-over, then bounced the other way, pretending to check the score on the Sox game. Mariah pulled me close, her hair smelling like an ashtray outside a mall. We talked about Sadie, her new preschool with the Playskool house out back, her new heart-shaped handbag. Mariah said she could speak in sentences and I asked her to tell me which ones. Whatever Sadie had said, I'd taught her to say it.

"I don't know," Mariah shouted against the techno. "I can't remember."

She laughed recklessly without making a sound. Then she went dead-eyed, killed her drink, and that was it. There was no conversation left to strain. Still, I wanted her close. There was something I badly needed to check. I pulled her neck to mine like we were conspiring, or Siamese, then stuck my mouth to her ear.

"I'm your angel?"

# I'M EXAGGERATING

SERENA WORE A NAVY two-piece suit, sensible flats, twisted-up hair, a buttoned collar over the wrist—read the faded *blah blah blah* script. Her first flight was to Wichita, and she had asked Niko if he knew what Wichita looked like from the sky. She wanted to hurt him. For him to picture her cloud-height, off the ground, sixteen hundred miles to the middle, untouchable.

She scooped ice and twisted bottle caps. Balanced her palms on headrests during dips. The aisle a tightrope. It rattled: the overheads, the ice, her fingers. Sometimes the pilot and the copilot looked like the cops who rapped on her door the month before. In the cockpit, their hands on the gears against the bright, complicated look of the control panel. The backs of their heads against the bright, complicated look of the sky. She cracked the front door, chain off the bolt, swollen eye. Her smile a cross, index finger against her lip. Niko was passed out in boxers, in the bedroom, in a deep sleep. The cops pushed through, ignored her.

"I made a mistake," she said. She paced, the blood in her hair graffiti orange and stiff. Blood on the white table, sprays of droplets from huffs where her mucus went loose under the break, her wrists twisted back.

"I'm exaggerating!" she told the cops, then recognized it as something he would tell her. Right in her ear like a basketball coach fighting the sideline.

"Get up," Niko would say. "You're faking all of this."

Wichita was not what she'd thought. Little Rock, Providence. Nowhere she'd been, or belonged, but all familiar. She had a day off in Spokane. Bumpy wheels of luggage by her heel, she roamed down Division Street, smokestacks spilling filth up towards an ocean-colored mountain. Janis Joplin on a brick wall, fingers outstretched. Towards the river, the smell of spoiled milk and a sign: Near Nature, Near Perfect. Pine trees that could see inside homes and for miles.

Back on the plane she found passengers to their rows. Locked in the Clorox blue of the bathroom, she fingered her new insignia, a wing pin she wore like a crucifix and to sleep. And on the dark seat, facing backward, going forward, she thought of what to do. This she thought of terminally. What was down there. What wasn't. There was no losing of a baby or liters of liquor in desk drawers.

Maybe there was a lost baby; to be exact is to lie.

She had enough money to run up a credit card. There was a lease, the stain of their signatures, one under the other. Hers under his, as if he could hold her down with ink.

Somewhere above Lake Superior she heard an infant's cry. It was a saltwater gargle, as disturbing and rangy as a vocal warm-up. She walked down the aisle, nearing the sound, and found a mother dozing in the seat. She lifted the infant from the sleeping mother's arms. Her T-shirt was splotched with milk at the nipples, her slump vaguely sexual, like she'd been slipped a mickey.

Serena strode the aisle with the infant in her arms, its wail an emergency. It filled the cabin with an engine-like force, though those fat-ringed thighs kicking against her stomach went nowhere. She watched as a businessman's eyes popped open. She gazed at them, felt his shock upon waking. Midair. Midshriek. She palmed the little one's wet head, the mask of a soft, wet scalp under her eyes. The seam of her lips by an ear the size of a bottle cap.

She whispered, "Hey there."

She whispered, "Don't be quiet."

She whispered, "Keep screaming."

# RAFFA

# WHAT COUNTS

I HAVE A CHANGE jar. Washed-out salsa jar on my windowsill. Pennies are there, dirty dimes, backs of my earrings, quarters for the subway if I'm desperate. I'm sifting through the change on the hardwood when Mickey comes in. He says, "Let's get everything."

In the supermarket, he steers with his backwards hat and the imprint of his wallet in his pocket.

"You like these?" he asks, then tosses chips into the cart. We stride down the aisle, kissing, but with his ten million arms whirling in more, like a fan in motion, I barely notice.

Later in bed, I try to talk to him about taxes. They take out a bit each month. But because his job selling insurance is better, a bit is big. "But isn't it relative," I say, "if everyone has to pay?" I can tell he's still thinking about it like a pie chart— what's missing— which reminds him to surprise me with some kind of next-level dessert soon.

But sometimes I have to admit: he looks good, with his fresh cut and his aviators and his Burt's Bees lips. No argument here. I'm waiting for him to come out of the dressing room in his tangerine pants. He looks so happy. Like there's a monkey on his shoulder. I can see him in his swivel chair.

"How do you pronounce BVLGARI?" I ask, fingering the glass over the glasses. Mickey says, "You don't."

I don't get it. It's like we're a special effect. I don't know why he brought us here. The lighting is low. I'm checking my savings under the table and it's not saving anybody. Mickey, like a tug on the wrist, a fast grab, says, "We're on vacation."

I say, "No, we're not."

We're confusing the waitress: "I'm great with water!" Mickey, through teeth: "Just get the drink."

I don't get it but I do.

On our walk home I say, "I'm picking up lucky pennies to embarrass you."

"Mickey, look, another one! One more."

I close my fist around the coins. Every second counts. Like before his company holiday party, our first fancy invitation on the fridge. Mickey comes in with a thirty and a few snowflakes on his shoulders. I'm clapping under my chin, in the kitchen by the ironing board. He kicks the door shut, then twirls me to the counter, where we crack beers, the iron hissing through teeth behind us, then burning. I turn Béla Bartók up on the speakers and say, "Mood music," when he asks what the hell this is.

He lays ties out on the bed, then me, his neck wet with cologne where I bite it. We fight for the shower, and the mirror, our arms scribbling on fast-forward with blow dryers, combs, and cans, holding out hangers and ChapStick. We twist to zip. He's mouthing, *We're late*, on the phone with the cab as he slurs our address, and I shrug, make like I'm slitting my throat, run over to squeeze him. He watches the clock on his wrist by the door as I click around with a blank look, searching for better heels, tearing through closets, tilting to stab earrings into closed holes. His whole Christmas thing is coming. I want more than he knows.

And then that night I have this dream. I'm squinting and I can see him, at the end of the aisle. With his skinny tie and his chewing gum and his tilted fedora. It's taken me twenty hours to get ready. Heel by heel, lash by lash, I go to him. The crowd gasps. We bow our heads to whisper, and negotiate.

For dinner, Rice Krispies, and every guest must take the SATs on a damp napkin. I forgot the DJ we hired was from New Jersey and the cake we bought was a burlesque show, as the photographer snaps him winking. A slow song comes on and the dance floor turns into a trap door, screams echoing endlessly down a baby's dirty mouth.

I yell in the cold parking lot, my voice carried away like a banner behind a helicopter. Just out of time, it comes back for me, the wind from the choppers blowing my dress up over my head. On the mountain, the seconds turn like the rain that's turned to snow. Nothing else to do but strip down and use myself. Make my heels ice picks to chip away and climb, noticing how things are from far and farther away.

# MICK'S STREET

I THROW THE KEYS at the mirror and they crash, a pitcher of water shattering during a high note. Applause-worthy. Mickey says I fight *ghetto*, and I always say, "That's right," like I'm proud of who I am.

"Why are you doing this?" I say.

"I'm not the one doing it," Mickey says. He nods to the pile of clothes beside the suitcase. What I hear is "the one." What I hear is the wind outside, snapping branches. Mickey says I'm a liar, that I hide things from him, from myself, too. He slips out a pack of 100s from his pocket, then slow-claps them against his palm.

"Going through my stuff?" I say.

"That's my suitcase, Raffa," he says.

What I hear is "my." What I hear is our wedding song, Elvis Presley. Mickey picked it and I panicked. New Year's Eve. I watched Serena's face till she blurred into Rima's, my head chained to his chest.

"You told me to leave!" I say.

I throw myself onto the bed and try to cry desperately into a pillow. It doesn't work, not at all. I hear him blending a protein shake in the kitchen. I want to be a list. Things that haven't been done yet on paper. Possibilities.

But then I pick up the keys. Mickey has a rental house on the Cape. We went there last winter and had sex in the loft, drunk and crying about things we'd never once talked about. I'd steal off to smoke on the porch, my hands shaking like Rima's, the keyholes of her fingers. I felt him watching me from upstairs.

Now Mickey's standing on the front steps in his huge parka with his hair slicked back like a real estate agent. I roll my suitcase past him. At him. Why has he done his hair for our breakup?

*Just get out,* Mickey mouths.

He runs forward to catch up. He's in sneakers, and I'm thinking that he's worn these on purpose, to chase after me.

Now that I'm going, Mickey shouts, "Where are you going?"

"I could run you over," I say, rolling down the window. Mickey throws his hands up. Then they're on his waist as I jerk the wheel, counting my luck that there's no one caught behind me as I swerve out. In the rearview he's already gone.

My car. The only thing in my name. One long stretch of highway, Xanax-smooth and soundless. The Cape, a weird place to go in winter. The Sagamore Bridge waiting in the distance. The water beneath it mirrors the sun, cracked as hairline fractures on X-rays. There's so much traffic, everyone honking and inching up. Profiles in the windows switching like a show of mug shots. I cross the bridge, pressing the window down for a smoke. The cold has teeth.

Cape houses are deceiving from the outside, little Monopoly pieces, all roof and rectangle. I'm carrying a twelve-pack of Heineken under my arm. I can smell my armpits even through my coat, some kind of hot sandwich with onions. I haven't showered since Friday, ever since Mickey sent me the divorce spreadsheet.

I remember the shrimp cocktail we ate, so fat the veins popped between my teeth. The night I said yes. And the way Mickey looked, self-possessed, satisfied. I snuck a cigarette out on the balcony. But where could I have crawled if not back to the table? If I were a movie, the credits would have been rolling up my face.

On the front drive, I take the wheezy steps of a Martian, sensing the quiet. Then I have to drop everything on the crushed shells of the driveway to search for the key Mickey leaves in the fake rock. The grass is cut but dead from the late

March snow. A green hose is hidden behind the bushes. Water trickles out of the metal head, a sound like gasping. The knob is freezing and it screeches as I twist it off. Below it is the rock, gleaming plastic, broken open. Someone's been here.

I knock the top off a Heineken on the kitchen island, size of a paddleboat and flecked with sparkling granite. If we get divorced, I'll get nothing. Maybe I'll get a couch, the piano Mickey bought but never plays. Where the fuck would I put a piano? I want a Steinway smashed through these floor-length windows so I can watch it hit, disturbing the skin of the lake.

On the dock, two boys with their backs turned are casting lines into the water. With their hoodies up around their heads, their figures are small and slumped as shepherds. From the dock, the path is soft dirt up the hill to the house. I'm not afraid of whoever has been here.

After I check the fridge, tuck my clothes into the stained oak drawers, bring the mound of newspapers inside, spread out the obituaries, then light a ghostly fire, I zip my coat and trudge down to the basement for a smoke. The glass glides open onto the gray slab, but the screen is torn and taped shut with Band-Aids. Fresh butts litter the edges of the concrete. Newports. I collect each one as I watch the boys, still standing with their backs to me on the dock. I shout to them and they turn, their hoods framing their faces.

"This is private property," I say, motioning to the floating raft they're standing on. The raft is anchored deep down in the muck. The lines are anchored to the boys, and their feet to the raft. The birds to the branches, their heads still as assassins. The boys gather their rods, leap from the dock to the shore, kicking sand on their way back up past the kayaks.

When they pass, I see their faces, one so pale he glows. He looks down at my hand, at the cigarettes jutting out of my fist. It's only when I'm inside that I see it, a backpack, slumped in the corner of the basement. It sits by the mantel, right under the antique Nude Beach sign with its arrow facing the lake. The bag is just there like a basket outside a church.

I pick it up by the shoulder straps, then stomp up the stairs. It's a black JanSport, jagged teeth for a zipper. I'm emptying its contents onto the kitchen island. I hold up an Angry Birds T-shirt, then bring it to my nose like I'm sniffing a carton of milk on the sour. It smells like wood chips and musk. I lay it flat.

In the front pocket is a crumpled pack of cigarettes. Newports, nine of them left. I splay each cigarette out under the shirt's sleeves, skeleton fingers with a pinkie missing. There's a pair of gardening gloves, and I scoop out candy wrappers and loose Band-Aids littered at the bottom, separating the Band-Aids from the candy and placing the wrappers in the palms of the stiff gloves. Two lottery tickets, scribbled silver at the scratch. I set them down, slide them as if across a Ouija board beneath the gloves. Backpacks are for addicts.

In the basement, I'm a PI. From here, I can see the curved wooden couch legs, electrical sockets. I crawl closer. There's a Samsung charger snaking out of the wall. I march back upstairs and pull open drawers at random. I drop the charger into a Ziploc, seal it shut, then hold it up to the light. It's just a phone charger. It goes straight onto the counter with the rest of the things. On the counter, the whole of the mound focuses into the shadow of a running man, a scarecrow smoking his own fingers.

Back downstairs, I pull on my winter driving gloves, which I never actually wear when I'm driving. The couch has a skirt and I flip it. It's damp and smells like Lysol. I reach out for a Coke can. In the natural light, it's dented and pocked, aluminum melted into a lip-sized hole. I seal it. It goes on like this: a side glance at a single-edged razor in an open puzzle box, gleaming there against all the colored pieces. Next to it, a torn Suboxone packet, which in my palm looks like a blue pack of two Advils you'd find in a hotel lobby, all the medical letters like a miniature résumé on the back.

When Benny overdosed, I found Suboxone wrappers crumpled and hidden in his closet. I studied the back, Rx only, then buried myself in his sheets. Once, numb from vodka, I brought Benny up with Mickey. There was a bread basket set between us, two knives. He told me to get over it. It'd been nine years since high school. He sipped his water at me, his eyes still, the ice rattling.

"Would you be over it?" I asked, even though I knew the answer. Mick makes so much money selling first-rate health insurance. He doesn't give a damn about anyone else's life.

It's not everything. I'm back on hands and knees, a beach crab. In the floral basement bathroom, the shower curtain is askew. Slumped on the tile is a white towel.
Under the sink, a spoon bent at the neck with a melted cotton swab in the center.
An empty foil blister pack of Percocet. An oversized Ecko jacket in the dryer, the
hood lined with sopping fur, folded aluminum tucked in the pockets, bright in the
center with a gleaming burn. I seal it with the last Ziploc.

A Heineken cap cracks against the counter and I slug it. I tuck the T-shirt
inside the Ecko jacket. Long arms, long torso, arms stretched out flat, cross-like.
Through the floor-length windows, the lake swirls a sunset, Nyquil pink and puls-
ing. I rearrange the squatter's stuff, put his cigarette finger up by his shirt's neck.
He'll be back. His things are here. I turn out the lights, the lake dividing itself into
darkness.

In the morning, I go for a drive. Where is this guy? He could be anyone, but not
anyone exactly. He's XL tall. I know that for sure. He buys lottery tickets. I pull
into the parking lot at Liberty Liquors. I stay an extra minute before getting out,
watch the clerk haul trash into the back bins. I have an insane thought. *Is that his
father?* I hoist my twelve-pack onto the counter. The checkout girl's bangs block
her eyes. It smells like powdered doughnuts in here.

"Is this it?" she says. I point to the Marlboro 100s. Then toss a Snickers into
the mix. The surveillance is grainy and slow. The trash guy comes back behind
the counter, and his neon vest flashes like a caution sign. He undoes the Velcro.

I drive all the way to the ocean and sit in my car. I chew the Snickers and tap ashes
out the window. I knew Benny was high when he ate sweets, but towards the end
it was better that way, seeing him at peace, the lifelines of his palm glowing orange.
Cheap off-season candy corn in the big bag, the waxy teeth in his palm. He'd eat
them one by one, eyes closed and red-rimmed.

I roll up the window. I lied before. The water scares me. It's different from the
lake, which stays the same. Maybe the squatter will be there when I get back. I'll
have to shut off my car a few houses down, tiptoe in. Maybe he'll be shooting up
in the shower, his hair dark and his tongue pearled in froth. His eyes too far gone
to look distraught when I kneel down to touch his cheek.

In my windshield, the clouds hang low. I'm not scared of addicts. Real estate agents terrify me. Housewives, cheerleaders. I turn up NPR so it feels like some-one is talking to me on purpose. Below, on the tiers of slate, the ocean rolls for-ward, a foaming mouth, then pulls back into itself. Such restraint. One more smoke. I roll the window back down a finger, tapping more ash onto the hardened sand of the lot.

I drive through Falmouth, unmarked roads. Trucks on blocks in driveways made of crushed white shells. Deserted restaurants, abandoned bookstores, old white churches, buoys on the lawns. A hangover starts late, the current blooming behind my eyes. By now I know my way around, so I'm just speeding down the narrow roads till I turn onto our street. Mick's street. Everything Mick's. I remem-ber when he held my hair up to his face with his fist after I swore I'd quit. You can only smell nicotine on people who aren't you.

"Can I have one thing to myself?" I asked, oddly weightless.

In the driveway, there's a truck. There's a truck. I leave my coat on the seat and click the door shut. A leaf blower drones in the backyard, the singular whine loudening as I climb down the path. Off by the trees, slimed leaves lift, then hurl themselves against the fence. A tall guy wearing sagging Dickies holds the blower like a wand, turning it back and forth over the grass. He has big headphones over an orange beanie like an air traffic controller. He doesn't see me. Then he does. I wave my arm out. The blower groans as the dust lifts into the air. A whiff of spring. I can't help it. I smile.

"Hey," I shout.

"What?" he says.

"You the gardener?" I say. He slips off his headphones, then his beanie. Over-sized diamond studs in both ears shine like a truck pulling up.

"You Mick's wife?" he says, swiping his hair back, tangled and tied. The leaf blower looks like a toy in his hand. The tarp on the grill flaps.

"I asked you first," I say. I'm not afraid. He is an animal cooperating pre-catch. I'm already walking down the path. The blower hangs by his side. The wispy hair on his chin resembles the fuzz on a tennis ball.

"I might be," he says. Boston draws up thick in his throat.

"You want to come inside?" I ask. He turns to face the lake, the wind picking up. A chime on the porch crashes hard.

"I have to finish up," he says. He swings the blower and points to the sand at the edge of the water, the leaves and broken branches trapped on the shore. "It's going to start raining like a bastard."

His bottom lip twists as the arrogant wind picks up. He's young. He thinks he knows how everything's going to go. A top tooth juts out against his bottom lip like a loose blind zigged against the row. He kicks up the blower, it roars, and then he turns again, his shoulder blades jutting from under his shirt. Leaves circle overhead. Down at the shore he revs it, annihilating the debris. And then the raindrops begin to prick, needling the length of my arms, then slipping fast through my fingers. I picture us inside as it storms, him on his knees, taping those Band-Aids down to my wrist. He cuts the blower like a murderer on Halloween as the rain makes a sheet between us. He struts his way up towards where I'm waiting at the sliding door.

I'm hiding my head in the fridge, rearranging bottles.

"I just have Heineken," I say. "And you left your things here."

I set two beers on the counter next to the stuff. His things spread into the distinct shape of a body outlined in chalk, the frame like a free fall. He stands looking out at the water with his hands punched into his pockets, his shirt dark with rainwater.

"Are you going to call the cops?" he says.

I walk behind him with a beer, then pick a clung leaf off his back. The belt loop of his sagging Dickies has come apart.

"No."

"I don't understand," he says.

"I do," I say. "You needed somewhere to stay?"

He smiles, a huff. "I don't have a place. Right now, I mean. I don't mean any harm."

"I don't, either." I hold out the beer. He looks down at my hand, then back up at me. He takes the beer and sits at the table, one leg out, his construction boots big and rimmed with dirt.

I join him, thumbing the side of my beer. "What's your name?" I say, twisting my hair up.

"Jordan," he mumbles.

"Where are you going to stay now?" He leans, his elbows on his knees, rubbing his palms together.

"Nowhere. In my truck. I'm from Bourne. Just up Route Six."

"I know where that is," I say. I read the obituaries. Cape Cod in winter. The land of overdoses. Cop bringing the same girl back with Narcan three times in one day. The narrow highway, empty liquor stores, the ocean swallowing hard as it draws back from the rocks.

"My boyfriend was an addict," I say. Jordan takes a swig, stays quiet. Breaking in, it's probably not the worst thing Jordan's done. I see Benny's clenched teeth, braces fresh off. His fist around a hammer and his palm flattened on the desk. The hammer *pounds pounds pounds*. I wait with him in the ER to score pills. Or in the parking lot at the pain clinics in New Hampshire, something to mend his anger. Driving home, waiting for the complete close of his eyelids, the jerk of the wheel to grab onto. I was a waiter.

"I was in sober living," Jordan says.

"What happened?"

"I don't know," he says. His palms shush together, eyes flitting from the counter to the door. "I stayed there awhile. I started working again at my buddy's construction company."

"That's hard work," I say.

"It's not. I like to be outside building houses, fixing roofs. Problem was his brother."

"Why?"

"I went over to his place just to see if I could be strong, not use. I guess that's not true. Junkie etiquette is that you don't shoot up a guy in recovery because you don't want them to wind up back like you—unless they ask twice."

"You asked twice."

At Al-Anon long after Benny died, I sat away from the circle in a church basement bubbling in the letters on the handouts. Women subdued, pink tissues damp in their clenched fists. And then they would start talking and they wouldn't for the life of them stop. Rage cut through my notebook, scribbling on its own like a lie detector test. I'd think, *You don't run out on people*. I'd think, *When someone is suffering, when someone you love is hurt, you go to them*.

"This place helped me let go of my son," a woman across from me said, her lips cracked down the center.

The wind overturned a kayak and rained twigs onto the grass. I have a life vest in my hands.

"Put this on," I say. We're outside the wet shed, the wood smelling like pencil shavings.

"Nah," he says.

"Fine," I say. "We'll do it your way."

We flip the kayak, then pull it through the oatmeal of the sand. The water ices up around my ankles till we leap onto the rain-splattered seats and push ourselves out into the lake. I've never been on a boat. The oars bump up against the plastic and the handles are heavy as trash bags. I think of a drain gasping dry and what's at the bottom of all this. But there's a glittering stillness when we stop, the boat spins in the center of the water, and we're far away from all the leaves and the trees and the houses. A low fog spills into the boat like karaoke smoke.

"It's nice out here," I say.

"I've come out here, like, every day, past two weeks," Jordan says, smiling. He's handsome when he smiles, like maybe if I turned his teeth back together one after the other, he'd have a chance.

"You just take the boat?"

He shrugs, chucks a tiny rock into the water, and it breaks the surface again and again until it stills. I want to tell him that you can't go home, how I wouldn't recognize home if I woke up in my childhood bed.

"This is my house, you know," I say. "This is my boat, these are my oars, and this is my fucking lake."

Jordan looks at me crazily and I break into a cackle. We laugh hard and I reach out and slap at the water. The two boys are back on the dock, their heads the size of pennies. They whip lines that fly riblike in white arcs, then sink. Even if I shouted, "This is private property! I'll call the police!" they would never hear me. The kayak starts to spin. I pull out a cigarette and Jordan reaches over. His lighter snaps and the flame is neon and surreal; it colors his face with a glow that isn't there. Mick said he'd divorce me if I didn't stop smoking. I won't and he will.

The wind picks up harder. Jordan reaches out his other hand to cover the light.

The boat bobs, gaining power, the water coming up over the edge, and then in one rough curve we're flipped. The cold is painless, at first. I swipe out to feel Jordan, slice my arms through the water, then open my eyes against the muck. Above is Jordan's sneaker, and when I grab hold he kicks, and the light sparks like power lines. We come up through the circle of water, choking and weightless. The water at the surface looks clear, like you could sip it if you were thirsty enough, which I am. Jordan's breaths are short, his eyelashes sparkling with beads of water. I wrap my arms around his neck. My thighs around his torso. Kiss his twitching eyelids like a mother.

Earlier, Jordan got up to go to the bathroom. I almost grabbed his arm. I was popping off another cap when he came back. He stood, looking out at the lake again. He laughed and it scared me. We faced each other on the dining room chairs. He was sweating through his hair. I saw it. His face looked like the delayed surveillance at the liquor store. He rolled up a sleeve and his forearm was scratched and purpled.

"Did you get high?" I whispered. I started to cry.

"Yeah," he said. His eyes swung lazily.

"Why didn't you tell me?" I said. I was in tears, and crazy.

His head bobbed back. He took me in with a squint and sucked in his breath. "Shit. I don't know," he said. "Sorry?"

"You're not sorry," I spat.

"You're kind of freaking me out," he mumbled. "Are you going to call the cops?"

His eyes flickered, chlorine-shot like he'd been staring at a penny for days on the floor of a pool. He was ruining it, this fight. Outside the rain slowed and I reached for his shoulder. I swept my hand up the solid curve beneath his T-shirt, then pressed my thumb to his neck, felt his pulse jump.

"I would never do that," I said, my thumb unmoving. When the cops found Benny slumped against the tile in a Laundromat bathroom, he was two hours dead.

I looked up at Jordan. "Shoot me up?"

The pressure from my thumb remained even as the beat from his neck raced on and on, then broke in a twitch.

"No," he said. "Let's go out on the lake."

But I asked twice. The lighter clicked under the spoon and the bubbles popped up tiny as Jordan flicked his wrist to shake them down. The kitchen filled with a sweet burning smell, candy in a bonfire. He took a Q-tip from his pocket and rolled it into a ball between his fingers, then sank the cotton into the bent spoon. The syringe drew up swirling and cloudy.

"Do some push-ups," Jordan said, so I got to the floor. Back on the chair, dizzied, he slapped the crook of my arm. I watched as my blood drew up dark, Jordan's lips by the needle. For a second I was stunned, something warm siphoning up my throat. I threw up, spit and beer all over Jordan's shoes. Later, on the floor, the sun was out, my head was pricked with warmth, but it was just Jordan's fingers in my hair.

We swim to the dock, which sways afloat. The boys are gone. I'm sure of it now. We kneel on the raft, our clothes hissing out streams of water from all sides like piss. I tilt back my head. The sun warms my neck and spins little rhombuses on the surface of my hands. We jump off the dock onto the starch of the sand.

The house waits for us as we trudge up the hill. Inside, beer, a fire, the warmth. A place to stay, though I'm more afraid than ever. Our sneakers squeak muck. I peel off my sweater and it slaps onto the concrete.

"Fuck," Jordan says. He's pulling on the back slider but it's good and locked.

He pounds on the glass. He pounds and pounds. I tilt my face back, feel the specks of sun but can't slide inside its center. Its warmth caught and laced through branches. Anything out here could happen, the March rain switching back to snow. Even sheltered, the homicidal birds that own the trees call out into the void as though possessed.

# RUN FOR YOUR LIFE

I WAS RUNNING FAST down Comm Ave when I saw the bike theft. Some kid in a hoodie had cut the lock. That cutting part I imagined. What I did see was a concierge outside the Eliot pulling the bike back from the kid like a tug-of-war. By this point I was running in place. I could run ten miles now. From my apartment, all the way across the BU Bridge, deep into downtown through the Common, then back again. I had skaters' calves, tight and glistening, like nylon. I was the only one who saw.

The kid looked confused, then directly at me, pulling the bike from the concierge. He was committed. He had already broken the lock. He yanked it hard and it bounced off the sidewalk as he hopped on, then flew right through the intersection on Mass Ave. There was a green light and I felt something terrible happen before it happened. I put my hands to my ears before he was hit. I watched the light turn yellow and felt the heat of the sun on my hair as the crash turned metallic, something skidding and crunched twisting through my ears like a corkscrew.

By now there was a crowd, a kid on the street in the middle of the intersection, and the lady whose car he hit leaning over him. She was in an MBTA public transit uniform, which made me think the police might come faster, though the two are not connected. The kid leapt up, as if by CPR, out from where someone could have outlined his body in chalk. The MBTA lady said, "Hey!" as he picked up the broken bike and spun it around, trying to make it go in a forward motion. The lady grabbed his arm and shouted, "Look what you did to my car!"

The kid wasn't listening. He was getting ready to run.

The lady kept one eye on the kid as she circled her dented car with a phone to her ear. A couple men in business suits had wandered into the street, keeping a hand on the kid's shoulder, murmuring things to him as if they were already his lawyers. The kid squinted up into the sun, and I imagined him saying to himself, "Fuck!"

Like that, just as I thought, he spun out of the men's grip like he was dribbling a basketball through their legs. He abandoned the broken bike. I don't know what to say about what happened next, other than it was automatic. I've been training for a whole year. I beat myself against my own time, every time. I don't miss a day.

I ran, the same route I run anyway, the sidewalk all the way down Comm Ave. It couldn't be a straighter line. From behind us, I heard the MBTA lady shout, "Get him!" and it blew like a whistle through my ears.

The kid had speed but I had purpose. He was done for. I was motored by the slick machinery of rage. The kid didn't know me, but I was his nightmare. I was going to catch him. Our bodies would collide, we'd trip into a fountain in the Common. I'd keep him down in the shallow water, his shirt dark and ballooning from below. I could feel the twitch like it was my own, his body fitful under my grip. And when I pulled him up by the throat, he would recognize my murderous eyes on the worst day of his life. What then would he have to say for himself?

He dashed through more green lights and I was closing in, darting through traffic, past brownstones and Marlborough Street, the trees flicking symbols of light off his back. I don't know what to say about what happened next, other than it was unrehearsed. I was getting close. Close enough to tap his T-shirt. Then I saw the frame of someone who looked like my ex-husband nearing. He was walking towards us, five parked cars away down the sidewalk. He was wearing Jesus sandals and a button-down, his hair faded on the side in that new Nazi cut.

It was my ex-husband. I knew what Mick would think of me before we made eye contact, his knowing green eyes all over me, then gone, going the other way. I didn't stop running.

After he tried to divorce me, I broke into his Cape house and did heroin for the first and last time. I threw my lighter at his second-floor window till he let me in. I went to the Gallows on a Wednesday. I took seven shots of Maker's. I texted him I was pregnant. When he didn't believe me, I threatened to murder him. It only led to us having sex for the last time. I hacked into his email, showed up to his friend's bachelor party, and chased him down the street after he told me to never, ever call him again. I did call him again, after he changed his number.

Now I am running after the boy, in flesh-colored spandex like I'm naked, and it's the first time we've seen each other since last year. I thought about stopping and explaining everything. This kid stole a bike. I started running last June. I'm not crazy. I'm trying to be a hero. But I didn't know how to quit anymore. Even if I did, I wouldn't.

We've passed my ex-husband. It's easier to forget someone when you have a higher purpose. I was so close I smelled the cotton on the kid's T-shirt, and the sweat on his neck was close enough to lick. I made one last leap. It's the leap I make when I'm a second from home, a final "Take *that*." It was enough to get him. I'm not strong but the kid was out of breath by now, and I thought he was kind of impressed.

I held his waist as we took tandem huffs like a dilapidated prom photo. We took deep breaths until they slowed, and then it was just my heartbeat pressed to his back. The kid had his hands on his knees, and for a second, I wanted badly for him to look back at me. I unchained my arms from his torso and took a few steps back, hands on my hips. I waited, the sun making one of those swift disappearances. Then I let him go.

# ACKNOWLEDGMENTS

**THE FOLLOWING STORIES HAVE** appeared first, in different versions, as: "Frankie" in *Redivider*; "Cribs" in *SmokeLong Quarterly*; "Stage Four" in *New Ohio Review*; "Benny's Bed" in *Sante Fe Quarterly*; "How I Dance" in *Corium Magazine*; "Tell Us Things" in *Juked Magazine*; "California" in *Atticus Review* and *The Drum*; "English High" in *Literary Orphans*; "Good Job" in *New Delta Review*; "I'm Exaggerating" in *Tin House* online; "What Counts" in *Bartleby Snopes*; "Mick's Street" in *Gulf Coast*; and "Run for Your Life" in *Bartleby Snopes*.

Thank you to Min Jin Lee, the good people at the University of Pittsburgh Press—Maria Sticco, Alex Wolfe, Chloe Wertz, Amy Sherman, and Jane McCafferty—and Christine Ma.

Thank you to Jenn De Leon and Adam Stumacher, my writing parents, who showed me love and gave me direction. Pam Houston, who changed my life in one car ride by opening her world to me. Maryse Meijer, whose edits recalibrated my eyes and contained decades of lessons. Benjamin Percy, who gave me the best advice. My friends and readers and teachers, Lloyd Schwartz, Joe Torra, Vincent Scarpa, Nadine Kenney-Johnstone, Cady Vishniac, Amy Bond, Pam Zhang, Michelle Wildgen.

And Sara Cutaia—my sock, who has been through every draft, every stage of this book. Thank you for being so constant and true.

Thank you to Jim DeRogatis, the greatest boss ever. My teachers at Columbia College Chicago. Cohort Malört forever: Sara-Kate, Thomas, E.P., John, Neil, Tyrell, Alexandra.

Thank you to the Wesleyan Writer's Conference, the Juniper Institute, the Squaw Valley Writer's Workshop, the Tin House workshop, and the Writing by Writer's workshops, University of Wisconsin–Madison. My fellow fellows: Mary, Lucy, Emily, Aria, Chekwube, Natalie, Natasha.

Coach. Thank you for staying there in your ringside seat. For helping me make something.

The loves of my life: Esther, Tugce, Emili, Joey, Karissa, Meg.

My brothers and Miss. My father. My mother. The physical way you worked every day was the single most useful and beautiful thing I've ever seen.